The GUEST HOUSE
AND OTHER STORIES

BY THE SAME AUTHOR

The GUEST HOUSE
AND OTHER STORIES

KRISTJANA GUNNARS

Anansi

First published in 1992 by
House of Anansi Press Limited
1800 Steeles Avenue West
Concord, Ontario
L4K 2P3

Canadian Cataloguing in Publication Data

Gunnars, Kristjana, 1948–
The guest house and other stories

ISBN 0-88784-523-1

I. Title

PS8563.U55G8 1992   C813'.54   C92-093268-1
PR9199.3.G85G8 1992

Cover design: Brant Cowie/ArtPlus
Typesetting: Tony Gordon Ltd.
Printed and bound in Canada

*House of Anansi Press gratefully acknowledges the support of
the Canada Council, Ontario Arts Council and Ontario
Publishing Centre in the development of writing and
publishing in Canada.*

For Eyvind

Contents

. . . But he allowed himself to be swayed by his conviction that human beings are not born once and for all on the day their mothers give birth to them, but that life obliges them over and over again to give birth to themselves.

— Gabriel García Marquez, *Love in the Time of Cholera*

THE GUEST HOUSE

THE INTERIOR OF THE country was covered with a deep blue fog. No lights were visible. The small airplane ground through the clouds, droning and bouncing. The fuselage rattled in the heavy wind. Erling let his mind wander back to Rungsted in Denmark, his childhood home. Why had he left? Why had he come to this Arctic island to teach in a rural school? He saw before him his father's small bakery. The predictable customers clopped over the cobblestone village center. Old men on wooden benches chewed tobacco in the midday sun.

Every Sunday he used to see his grandparents for tea. They lived in a four-storey estate with a park that stretched in layers down to the beach. From their tower he could see lights across the channel in Sweden and freighters glide by into Copenhagen. There he had access to a telescope with which he surveyed the night sky.

When the plane landed in Reykjavík the students and teachers were met by relatives who looked weary from hours of waiting, drinking coffee out of machines and watching janitors mop the floors. Erling could hardly imagine a more depressing airport, especially at this time of year when storm and sleet lashed against the frail walls that shuddered and seemed to sway with the pressure.

It was cold. The linoleum floors, plastic countertops, chrome-plated stools and lounge chairs, rubber conveyor belt, were cold. Even the telephone, with the chilly voice emanating from the black plastic in his fist, was icy. As he waited for his cab, he observed the ritual of baggage claiming, trunk loading, the kissing and hugging of family members. Erling travelled light, his only possession a backpack. He was even freed from the burden of family. He did not need to account for himself to anyone.

The taxi arrived and Erling swept into the front seat. They drove slowly through the puddles in the old streets. Sleet hammered against the windshield and blowing snow dimmed the headlights. He could hardly see through the fury of the weather. They stopped in front of the tiny steps of a guest house on Snorrabraut where a dim yellow streetlight hung over the door.

After ringing the bell a light went on in the hall and the caretaker strode up the stairs from her basement suite. She opened the door with a large key and looked at him quizzically. In a moment her face burst with recognition.

"Oh yes," she exclaimed, "come in from the cold."

He stepped in, soaking and windblown.

"Your room is ready, just follow me," she said and headed up the stairs.

She was a dark woman from the Faeroe Islands who spoke Icelandic with a thick Faeroese accent. Her manner was warm and domestic. She opened the office with the key, wrote his name into the register and took his room key off the hook on the wall. Then she led him up the flights of stairs to the top floor and opened a small corner room on the left. Across the hall there was another, larger room, a bathroom adjacent to that and down the hall was a very small kitchen and a shower room at the end.

Erling recalled the details, the smell and sound. Unlike other guest houses he knew, this one smelled like a home. The caretaker drew the curtains, turned on the lamp and put his key on the table wishing him good night. When she was gone he shut the door and sat down in the easy chair. His bed was in the wall like a box, with curtains to shut out the room.

At last he was alone. At last. That night he slept with

a new sense of well-being, pleased to have the entire top suite to himself. There was no one in the other room so he could look forward to a week of privacy. He had not felt this peaceful since he left Denmark. The storm continued through the night as he slumbered in his attic room under the red-tiled roof of the guest house.

It was already ten when he awoke next morning. He had not slept this late for three months. It was still dark outside. He lazily got out of bed, washed and dressed. The sky was turning lavender as daylight filtered through the fresh and furry snow. Yesterday's storm had left the streets black and wet and snowflakes melted on the concrete. The city looked grey and raw.

He put on his coat and walked to a small food market on the corner. People bustled about on the streets, making ready for Christmas. He knew everything would shut down for the holidays so he returned with a week's supply of flatbread, smoked meat, sausage, herring and skyr. Back in the guest house he put his stock away in the kitchen cupboard. He was warm from the walk although the air was damp and a chill wind blew in from the sea.

That night he read while darkness poured into the narrow streets around the guest house. His copy of Kierkegaard felt tight and crisp in his hands. Except for the automobiles passing in the street below, there was no disturbance. He read by the lamp until fatigue consumed him and he slept in his alcove without drawing the curtains.

From then on day and night seemed to mingle together. He did not bother about the clock and felt free from the shackles of time that bound him at the school. Daylight appeared at eleven and it was dark by two. Life took place in a seemingly eternal night. At the school this fact depressed him. The darkness made the students drowsy and discipline was difficult to enforce.

Here it was different. Once the caretaker bustled in the adjacent room and the vacuum cleaner tore through the hall, but it did not last long. The day and night before Christmas passed easily and silently. Erling read, took long walks, and contemplated.

On the night of the twenty-fourth he was touched by a vague gloominess. Everyone else was celebrating and feasting. Large legs of mutton, bottles of wine and bowls of rice covered the dining tables in every house. Trees were lit up, presents torn open and psalms were chanted. It was always the same. He could smell roast pork from the basement.

His mind wandered to the repetitious ritual in his own house: the taste of soured red cabbage, the smell of burning wax and malt late at night. He had always wanted to spend Christmas without the decorum of habit and ritual, to see what remained when the holiday was stripped of its ornateness. And this was it.

When it was almost midnight a loud cry broke the silence. It sounded like a bleating lamb or a suffocating cat. Erling waited for it to stop but it grew more insistent. At last he got up, opened the door and looked into the hall. Everything was the same. The light was on and shed a dim radiance on the green carpet.

The cry could be heard from the guest room on the other side of the hall. It was a baby. He could tell from the sniffling and choking. Apparently someone had moved in there. He suddenly became ill-tempered: his solitude was broken and he would now be forced to share the kitchen and the bathroom. With a baby in the suite there was no certainty of peace.

Erling retired to his room again and shut the door. He tried to read but the crying of the baby continued. When it pitched, the noise was unbearable and he flung the book on the seat, swung open the door and strode across the hall. He knocked on the door. No one answered, but the crying became frantic. He knocked more forcefully, this time with his whole fist, but there was still no answer. At last he tried turning the doorhandle. It yielded to his touch. As he slowly opened the door he pattered on it gently with his finger.

The room was brightly lit. Baby clothes, diapers and

bottles were strewn around the room and a small crib jerked spasmodically in the middle of the floor. On a sofa near the window, a woman lay motionless. Her arm hung over the edge and brown hair covered her face and pillow.

Erling glanced at the baby and just as he did, it spewed a small fountain of vomit over its face. The child tried to swallow, but the vomit stuck in its throat. The tiny legs and arms frantically swung about and the chest gasped for air. He ran to the crib and picked up the baby. It seemed to be suffocating and its face was turning purple. He turned it upside down, held it by the ankles and slapped it on the back until the throat cleared and the child caught its breath. Then he cradled it in his arms.

At first the child's eyes were large and terror-stricken. He paced about with the baby and approached the body of the woman. She was not dead as he had feared. An overturned bottle of vodka lay on the table and a glass stood on the floor by the sofa. She had evidently passed out. He tried to rouse her but she seemed lost in a deep sleep.

He picked up the glass, still holding the baby, but did not know where to put the glass. The baby was crying less severely and rested its warm head on his shoulder. It felt like jelly in his arms. He was afraid of pressing too hard or letting the heavy head slide for fear it might fall off. The unpleasant smell of vomit and the stench from the soiled diaper were an entirely new phenomenon to him. The sleeves and sides of his sweater soaked up the child's wetness.

Not knowing what to do next, he decided to take the infant to the caretaker. He made his way down the stairs with difficulty, holding the baby awkwardly with one arm and clasping the railing of the stairs with the other. When he reached the basement he rang the doorbell to the caretaker's apartment and patted the child's back as he waited. He could see the woman's familiar form appearing behind the curtained window in the door.

When the caretaker opened the door her eyes shot wide open and her hand flew over her mouth.

"Pardon me," Erling stammered, "excuse me for disturbing you, tonight of all nights."

Behind her he saw the disarray of the evening's celebration. Organ music flowed into the stairway from her living room.

"There seems to be something wrong upstairs," he explained, stammering slightly.

The caretaker had discerned the situation by now and extended her hands to Erling in an offer of lightening his load.

"Is this the child from your floor?" she gasped as she took it. "Oh my God, will you look at this. Solveig, come here. Dear God."

A young girl with long black braids appeared and the baby was handed to her.

"What happened?" the woman asked, turning her attention to Erling.

"I don't know, really," he answered. "The baby was crying and since no one opened the door I walked in. I believe it was suffocating to death when I found it. It must be sick. The mother seems to be sick as well, or perhaps drunk, but she is not conscious as far as I can tell." Erling threw open his arms in his general confusion.

The caretaker did not wait for more of an explanation, but started up the stairs muttering under her breath. Erling followed. On their way up she whispered to him confidingly.

"She's an alcoholic. She just had the baby a few days ago. I put her in the room up there for we didn't have any other ones to spare. She has no one to go to." After a few heavy breaths from climbing up the stairs she added, "The city pays her bill."

When they entered the baby's room the caretaker immediately started to clear up. She covered the sleeping woman with a blanket and brushed her hair aside.

"Don't worry," she said reassuringly to Erling, "my daughter will take care of the child. We'll clean everything up. Thank you for coming down." She started for the door. "I'll get my daughters to help, don't you worry. Poor Ingibjörg," she half whispered and rushed awkwardly down the stairs.

Erling stood alone by the door of the stranger's room. The woman still lay motionless, her face as pale as the pillow. Then he returned to his own room. The bustling of the caretaker and her two daughters continued far into the night. He heard their low voices and occasionally the baby sounded through the whispering.

The night's experience had completely altered his mood. He had saved the baby's life, he was convinced of that. The thought shook him. When he pictured the suffocating child, sweat broke from his forehead. He neither read nor slept, but paced the floor in restlessness. At last, towards morning when the movement in the hall had ceased and all was quiet again, he lay down and watched the gleaming night sky through the window. The stars were large and the northern lights spread like orange and green curtains across the firmament.

Next day the caretaker's daughters could be heard shuffling through the hall now and then and the baby's crying occasionally disturbed the barely audible movement in the other room. When Erling went out and returned he sometimes caught a glimpse of the retreating shadow of the young girl with long braids. Once she passed him in the hall carrying a warm bottle of milk. He never saw the baby's mother and the child was also confined to its room behind closed doors.

On the twenty-sixth he met the caretaker in the entranceway as he was leaving for a walk. He asked her how the mother and child were doing.

"You know, she does absolutely nothing but lie in bed," the Faeroese woman confided to him. "She drinks all the time. My daughter takes complete care of the baby and cleans the room. She even has to clean the mother. Poor Ingibjörg. And they want to remove the baby, I get visitors asking about Ingibjörg but I can't tell them the truth. If they knew, the child would be taken away and Ingibjörg would never forgive me. How can I be responsible for having a child taken from its mother?"

Erling did not know what to say but he agreed she should probably keep silent and wait to see what happened.

Next day he met the caretaker again and she came rushing to him with a beaming face.

"Guess what," she whispered excitedly, "Ingibjörg has stopped drinking." She folded her hands and looked at him beaming with pride. "She threw away all her vodka and she has worked hard all day, I'm so proud of her."

That night Erling paced confusedly through the city streets where snow was melting on the sidewalk.

Warmer temperatures broke up the ice and the streets were slippery.

On the following day Erling suddenly realized that much of his food supply was missing. He had calculated his need precisely and now he saw he would not make it through the vacation. When he came into the kitchen that evening he found Ingibjörg in the act of stealing some of his flatbread. The long knitted house-coat she wore made her look tall and slim. Her fingers clutched a partially eaten flatcake.

She stood motionless and without expression for a moment when she noticed Erling. Then she tossed the bread haughtily on the counter and paced out. He meant to speak to her but she slammed the door to her room before he could catch up with her. Returning to the kitchen he thought the situation over. Ingibjörg obviously had no opportunity to buy food before she came to the guest house: she was at the hospital. She must be starving.

He strode back down the hall and knocked forcefully at her door. There was no answer. He knocked again and a hoarse voice answered "Come in."

Erling opened the door. Ingibjörg sat on the sofa with her face turned towards the window. He cleared his throat to speak and she looked at him.

"I just wanted to invite you to eat the food that's in the kitchen," he said awkwardly. She stared at him but did not answer. "I want you to eat my food," he repeated, this time as if he were assigning homework to a class.

"I have never yet been a beggar," she replied coldly and turned to stare out the window again.

"May I invite you to dinner then?" he asked.

"Feel free if you want to," she answered curtly without turning around.

Erling returned to the kitchen and prepared tea and sandwiches which he arranged neatly on a tray and carried back to the woman's room. She still sat in the same spot when he entered.

"I made some tea," he explained as he set the tray down in front of her.

"I don't drink tea," she muttered, still expressionless.

He was about to speak but she interrupted.

"Thank you anyway," she added.

"Please eat," he said, motioning to the food.

She grabbed the bread and ate it greedily without a word. He poured her some tea. After considering for a while, she reached behind the sofa and pulled out an open bottle of vodka. She bit into a sandwich and studiously poured the alcohol into her tea. Then she spiced his tea as well before he could stop her.

"I'm sorry," he excused himself, "I don't drink." Thinking better of it he added, "But I'll keep you company with this one cup."

They ate and drank in silence. He let her finish the food and while she ate he stood up and looked at the sleeping infant in the crib. It was clean and seemed well fed. Ingibjörg resupplied her tea and drank it while observing Erling coldly.

"Where is the father?" he asked, turning around.

Ingibjörg sat as if turned to stone on the sofa. She held her cup stiffly, took a sip from it without moving her eyes away from him. Her expression was haughty, almost arrogant. Erling suddenly felt he had offended her. He was awkward.

"You're not from around here, are you?" Ingibjörg suddenly said hoarsely.

Erling shook his head. They sat in silence. The clock in the hall struck the hour. He tried to count the rings but forgot the numbers. He felt hot and uncomfortable. Ingibjörg began to laugh haughtily. Her cold voice broke into a cough.

"Do you want to hear a story from the country?" she said. "Perhaps you should hear one of the stories from up north," she repeated, looking at him as though he were a youngster. He was confused.

"Once there was a naughty boy who refused to recite his 'Our father'," she went on without waiting for his answer. "He was spanked but he wouldn't say the prayer. Then he was spanked again but he still wouldn't say it. Finally he was spanked for the third time and a blue fog rose from the boy's head. After that he recited his 'Our Father'."

With this, Ingibjörg leaned back, stretched her neck and laughed loudly.

After that she said nothing. She finished the food in silence and Erling waited while she ate. He could think of nothing to say. He noticed that Ingibjörg was very pretty. Her shoulder-length brown hair fell in waves around her face. Her eyes were dark, nearly black. Her lips were bright red. Her fingers were long and the fingernails had old nail polish on them. A little later he left the woman and infant in their room, cleaned the plates and cups, and went for his usual walk in the dark streets towards the airport and the university.

The woman across the hall continued to steal his food the next day but he did not see her. On the thirtieth he knocked on her door to tell her he was leaving. His plane was scheduled to fly that evening. No one answered the door. He went down to the caretaker and asked her where Ingibjörg was. The Faeroese woman stepped out into the hall, closed the door behind her and whispered to him.

"She's been taken away."

"Taken away?" Erling repeated, incredulous.

"Yes, to an institution," the caretaker whispered again.

"But why?" Erling protested.

"To a mental hospital," she said hastily, hushing him

down. "She couldn't take it, poor girl, she was beside herself every time someone asked to adopt the baby. She thought everyone was after her child. Yesterday when you were out, she had an attack of nerves, poor girl, and the police had to come for her."

Erling was dumbfounded.

"She didn't seem disturbed to me," he insisted as if he could change the situation. "I saw her just two days ago. She isn't mad, there must be a mistake," he insisted.

"They had to fight tooth and nail to get the baby off her hands," the woman added sadly.

"You mean they took the baby?" Erling asked incomprehensibly.

"Yes, it went to her brother's" was the answer. "She was unfit to keep it. She couldn't do it, poor thing, and she didn't know it herself."

"But they can't do that without her consent?" he argued.

"They can," the woman assured him. "She isn't well. Her liver is damaged."

Erling felt as though he had been hit by a rock.

"But the child," he protested almost to himself, "it was MY child."

The words blurted out of him before he knew what he was saying. The Faeroese woman's eyes shot open and she looked at him strangely for a while.

"Your child?" she said hesitantly.

"Yes!" he insisted. "I mean," he began to stammer, "I saved its life so in a way I gave it life. They can't simply remove it."

"They did, though," the caretaker assured him. "You know, it's the third time and she's proven herself incapable."

"What do you mean, the third time?" Erling whispered.

The woman answered confidingly: "She's had two other babies who are fatherless and were adopted because she couldn't take care of them. I think losing a third one was too much for her. She snapped."

Erling left the guest house feeling unexpectedly dazed. The warm weather had given way to crisp frost. The streets were still. Even the usual breeze from the harbor was missing. He walked to the airport thinking the fresh air would lift his spirits. His shoes broke the thin ice on the puddles. The sidewalk was cracked into giant cobweb designs. He looked at the city as if through glass.

When he entered the terminal he was tired from the long walk and let himself fall into the plastic chair. Familiar faces of students and teachers greeted him. The fresh young people were beaming with energy from the holidays. They appeared to him coated with an almost angelic haze. The loudspeaker announced the boarding of his plane. He stood up and started for the line. He stepped aside to let all the young people filter through the narrow door into the darkness outside where the plane waited. Taking a deep breath he followed.

WATER

SURE ENOUGH, AS THE DAY of her departure drew near
the weather changed. After a beautiful summer of
sunshine, swallows, squirrels, crab apples, robins, in-
sects, yes it was now raining. All those living beings had
found places to hide. The rain pelted down in torrents
at night, beating up on parked cars and "For Sale" signs
on front lawns as if there were vengefulness in the sky.
When she walked to the corner travel agency, just to
have a photocopy made, just a few paces, her tennis
shoes were soaking. She might have been walking *in*
the river, the Red, that flows by her house under the
Maryland bridge. But it was the street, not the river,
and it was raining.

She had to get up at night and close all the windows
in the sunroom. Those enormous windows, as large as

herself almost. To open and close them, she had to stride from one end of the room to the other. The windows were the pride of the summer. Behind them she followed the season at her leisure. That was the important thing: *at her leisure*. No one walked unannounced into a sunroom the way people walk into a garden: the paperboy, the courier with Federal Express letters to sign for. The bricklayer: "I wanna inspect the bricks to see how to clean 'em, the lady called." Not into the sunroom. Here she had privacy. Something the world knew.

The rain these days. She could only describe it as *enormous*. So enormous that it kept her awake at night, the water, not drops but water pouring, attacking the walls of her house at the angle of the wind. Through the glass she saw the trees bending down under the force of wind and water, trying to raise their crowns but never succeeding. And the clouds: the clouds moved so fast she did not believe they were clouds. She had to peer out to make sure they were: the clouds were charging from east to west. *Charging*. Something furious was going on in the weather system. And noise. Rain like car engines humming all along the street, left in neutral, emergency brakes engaged, the drivers all abandoning their cars without turning them off.

And what really crackled her of course was the lightning. Thunder that always accompanied these rainstorms on the prairies. It never just rained: it rained and thundered. The two went together like love and marriage. She lay at night in her volumes of pillows and duvets, in the dark, not sleeping because the thunder cracked everywhere. Not just outside her window, but all around town. She could follow the blasts, like bombs during an air raid on the city, firing off in various places. She found herself thinking: the ruins of the United Church on Furby have been hit *again*. The hospital, hope the hospital has not been hit, patients scrambling out of high beds, untying tubes from various devices leading into their bodies.

It often occurred to her, not just now during a prairie rainstorm, but often, that public perception of meteorological phenomena should be *fine tuned*. This was not a European rainstorm. This was a torrent. Why do the Monsoons of South Asia get all the press? The flooding of the Nile in Africa? *The rainy season*, they say, when there is a wind from the Indian Ocean. During the Monsoon, the wind blows *from the southwest*, bringing with it the rains. This is a Monsoon: it is seasonal, it floods cities and acres and highways. Cars driving along a road that encounter *this* Monsoon are, for all practical purposes, headed for the river. They dive headlong into an ocean of water that suddenly fills the streets. All the parts of a conventional automobile are instantly soaked, the engine turns off and the driver has

to abandon the car with the hood up saying "I give up."
White flag. Truce.

And yet, with all that water — the rains in summer,
snows in winter — the prairies are *arid*. High and dry.
Not being at sea level, the prairies are a high plateau
flattened by glaciers of a distant past and subject to the
thick, dry winds of higher altitudes. The soul in the
prairies is dry. People head for the lakes, of which there
are many: depressions left by those old glaciers and
filled with water *from above*. Even when it rains people
gravitate to Lake Winnipeg, Lake Manitoba, if only to
watch the tinselly drops at the margins of rainstorms
tickle the silt grey water of the shallow lakes. They throw
themselves into the water to be rained on level with the
flat surface of the lake. A natural silk sheet, a waterbed.

Even during a Monsoon they go to the lake. Highways Eight and Nine from the city going north fill up
with cars. Cars with small boats on top, windsurfing
platforms, water skis. Canoes. As the gravedigger said
about the dead: *they head for the trees*. When she was
selecting a gravesite, not for herself, but selecting, she
asked for a spot under an oak tree. "That's what they
all want," the gravedigger said: "when they heard we
were opening this new cemetery where there were oak
trees, *the trees drew them like magnets*. One lady said my
husband's gotta be under a tree, he was a logger and
wouldn't feel right out in the open. I said, lady, I

wouldn't wanna be under a tree if I was a logger by God *it was a tree that got him in the first place*, a fallin' tree that killed him why I'd wanna be as far from a tree as possible."

When she was a radio journalist she went up there, to the lake. It was summer, like now, and rains. They were working on a lake story and she had the cameras on her. When they arrived in Gimli harbor the skipper, the one they were trying to get for an interview, said he couldn't. He had to pilot a family out to the middle of the lake. They wanted to spread a man's ashes over the waters: a fisherman, spent his life fishing Lake Winnipeg, was to be spread on the water. The pastor was coming, the wife, the children. You can come too, he said, and they did.

It was a hazy day, she remembered that, and the highway out of the city particularly grey and industrial looking. Junkyards, sausage factories, railyards, abandoned warehouses on Highway Eight. At least on Highway Nine there was a winery, a major park in Kildonan, a number of Ukrainian Orthodox Churches with onion domes pointing at the F.P. Grove clouds sailing overhead on a good day. And an old historic fort, Lower Fort Garry, with caked mud-colored walls surrounding whitewashed buildings containing fox skins, beaver pelts, hanging on hoods under the roof. Young people in costume playing Governor or scullery maid or Governor's mistress, trying not to indulge in gossip when uppity high school kids ask pointed questions about sexual liaisons at the Fort. Over a hundred years ago today.

From Highway Nine they took a right turn and dove, more or less, into the lake town of Gimli. Unlike other prairie towns, Gimli suddenly is there, like the bottom of a lake when you dive down: all of a sudden very close, and you thought the lake was deeper than that. Most other towns around here announce their presence miles before you arrive. Because of the view: because you see everything an hour before you get to it. But at Gimli the land is so bushy with trees and shrubs that if you do not read road signs you do not know where you are. You do not see it. They headed for the harbor where they quickly located their boat, tied to the dock. *Frón* it was called, something like that, and an Icelandic skipper.

She did not remember the name of the skipper: it was Jón or Sigmundur or some such. He was a fat man with a pilot's cap, a ruddy face and an enormous navy-blue winter jacket. It's cold out here, he said to them, *threatenin' to rain*. In that peculiar Icelandic accent they all have up there, even those who never set foot on Iceland and who *do not even speak Icelandic*. There is an accent in the interlake that passes for an Icelandic accent but is really a dialect of Canadian English, she thought. Sigmundur the skipper, it turned out, had a little cabinet on his boat where he kept a little whisky. He invited them up for a *heart warmer*, he called it, because it gets a little cool out there. Her colleague, the fellow with the recording equipment dangling on his shoulders, went up with the skipper. She stayed on the deck, prowling about the boat, looking for descriptions, watching the foam of the lake water between the boat and dock.

A friend of hers up here, a fisherman named Gudmundur, had just lost his boat. There was a rainstorm that year, a week or so before they went up for the lake story. Like today, overcast, small tinselly drops starting to fall, which later turned into torrents. The rains came pouring down so suddenly that fishermen did not have time to pull nets out of the lake. One fishing boat capsized in the storm, a crew member going down and drowning. They could not find his body, even after scouring. The coast guard, or lake guard, turned out to be useless. When they were called on, the fishermen discovered they were just *city high school kids hired for summer jobs* and did not know the first thing to do. Her friend Gudmundur's boat was tied up at the harbor, but *it rained so hard that the boat went down*. Right there, in the harbor, the boat so filled with rain that it sank.

Soon the bereaving family arrived at the boat: an

elderly, white-haired, thin woman with a horseshoe-shaped mouth was escorted silently up the ramp onto the deck of the boat by a tall, thick, dark-haired younger man. A son perhaps, or son-in-law. Then another man, a bit wider in the girth, and two middle-aged women. There may have been more but she did not remember. Sigmundur skipper came out and told them all where to settle themselves: the two couples up front, the widow on a chair under a roofed-in, open area next to the wheelhouse. There she sat on a folding-chair holding a plastic bag filled with ashes. Her husband. On her lap. Then the red-haired pastor from the local Lutheran Church came, wearing a casual Sunday suit and a pleasant smile.

They untied the boat and sailed out onto the lake. She leaned against the balustrade, over the water, as they sailed along the lengthy pier where individuals sat holding long fishing poles over the water. She had seen them there, often sitting all day, catching small lake fish. People from the city who otherwise go golfing on Sundays, Saturdays, and weekday afternoons if their jobs were particularly high ranking. Sometimes they simply would not go to work at all, but to the golf course. Government employees: Deputy Ministers, ADMs, who phone in to their secretaries at nine a.m. *Gone fishing.* The show could go on without them, surely it could. Medical frauds, airplane manufacturing contracts, potash sales to India: they could wait. Postal strikes, nurses' strikes: let them wait.

Eventually they were out on the lake and the sounds of land had receded behind them. A certain peace overtook the soul out there: a sense that finally there is water. Like when the starved bee suddenly flies upon a garden full of *clovers*, clovers by the thousands in the grass. Water all around, and also threatening to come down from the sky. The lake was so large that however far you sailed, you would not see the other side. It was a sea: a Mediterranean on the prairies. That often occurred to her in fact, not just that day on an ash-strewing expedition when the lake seemed particularly large. But often. Why did the Mediterranean get all the press? What about Lake Winnipeg? This was no European small sea with merchant ships passing one another en route between continents with curry, cayenne pepper, silkworms on board. But a prairie ocean with fishing boats loaded with pickerel, lake trout, Winnipeg goldeye. Going down in the storm, *no less than in a storm on the Mediterranean*. Death is death, everywhere, no matter where, she thought. *Death on the Mediterranean, or in Venice, was, in principle, no more significant than death on Lake Winnipeg.*

They sailed so far out on the lake that land was not visible on any side. The horizon was silk grey. She thought of a ditty from her childhood, perhaps something she was made to recite at school. She no longer remembered the poem. It was called "Water." She stood up behind her desk and recited to the class: *Water . . . you have no color of your own, Heaven's hue you borrow.* And here all that distinguished water from sky was a thin grey line, faintly outlined by some tired artist to indicate this was where the lake ended and the overcast sky began.

Sigmundur skipper turned the engines of the fishing boat off. The vessel floated silently on the water, not undulating or heaving. Not like a ship on the North Atlantic that glides up on billows that have begun in the depths and then dives down when the ocean flattens again, *worse than a roller coaster* she remembered thinking as a child on those ships, more awesome. This fishing boat did nothing except course a bit in the direction of the wind as it stood alone on the lake. Perhaps the wind was coming from the southwest that day. A slight wind, but slight winds on the lake could easily become storms. She knew that all along. A storm on a shallow lake is another word for disaster. A storm on a shallow lake that whips up the thin water and swallows all that is in and on it gives new meaning to the word *drowning*. She knew that. They all knew that.

The pastor helped the thin widow with the horseshoe mouth out of her chair and over to the railing farther front on the boat. He took the *plastic bag* from her gripping hands and untied the *wire* that kept the ashes from falling out. It was like something they had bought at Safeway, she remembered thinking, or at Superstore, where you shovel up your own scoops of flour or sugar or brown sugar or oats, *into a plastic bag that you close with a small thin wire*. The pastor said something she did not hear, but sounded like part of a psalm. The group of relatives sang a short hymn. Then the pastor *overturned the bag* as he held it over the water. He did not put his hand in and spray the contents, ashes, over the water in an inspired gesture of poetic sorrow. Instead he turned the bag over and *dumped the ashes into the water*. She thought ashes were light as dust and flew in the wind, unable to find enough gravity to actually *land*. But these ashes were heavy: heavy as lead. They fell into the lake with a thud.

Very quickly the skipper turned the engine on again and began the turn around to head back to the pier. Her colleague had apparently been in the wheelhouse with him getting a head start on the interview. Over another swig. The young journalist with gold hair — all people here were Icelandic it seemed — emerged from the wheelhouse with a smile on his face. And a glint in his eye. They had taken a glass during the *funeral*, which was not the right word for what had just passed, she was thinking. He went around with the microphone, taking up the sounds of the boat as it sailed. The engine noise. The wind on the deck. The water broken by the keel. She took the microphone when he handed it to her, leaned over the railing, over the water, held the microphone down as far as she could reach. Recording the water of the lake: where Sigmundur lived his life piloting his fishing boat.

There were the hours preceding a rainstorm, when the air was charged with electricity. People went about with a strange feeling. An unidentified feeling. They could not account for it, but *something was wrong*. Tempers rose to a higher pitch. Sensitivities tightened. Eyes became watchful, not exactly suspicious, but with suspicious looks nonetheless. Old people complained of *light-headedness*. Fat people claimed to have *arthritis in the knees*. Babies in cribs suddenly felt *ticklish*. Young men found themselves asking their new wives: is it your period? Then, with the first flash of lightning in the air, the first clap of thunder, people straightened up and said: ah! It's the thunder, of course. *You know dear I always feel this way before a thunderstorm.*

And other hours after a rainstorm. Exhausted hours. People did not really know why they were so *tired*. The sky was overcast. *It's such a dreary day.* Even the golf course was almost empty. The green elms were dark green, the crab apple trees orange instead of yellow, the birds and squirrels suspiciously out of sight. Against the lead grey sky, moss green crowns of trees shook and wriggled in the remnants of storm. Streets were still wet, cold dark stretches on the pavement where automobiles slowly started up again, one by one. Walkways were filled with puddles. Runners were unable to jump over them so they resorted to walking. All metallic objects outside were washed clean. Windows, cars, kiddie wagons, lawn chairs: clean.

And it was time for her departure. All rains, all storms, lakes, events, seasons, have their end. She was leaving a wet city behind, wet acres in the country, farmers crying for *no rain, just while we harvest*. But the weather system always did operate without regard for human needs or desires. And there was a new story, besides, on the water, which she was no doubt going to have to look into. To *record*, in a way: cyanide in the prairie ponds north of the city. It was discovered that someone had dumped cyanide into a pond in *Bag Bay*. That was only six miles from the intake of the city's *drinking* water. She imagined turning on the tap, taking a glass of water: and that would be that. The end of the story. It was a real question to ponder: who would find her there? After all, everyone in the city would have *imbibed* the *same* water. Everyone would be on the kitchen floor, face down, one arm above the head, a broken glass in bits strewn over the floor to the right of the body. Water in a small puddle on the linoleum. *Water.*

THE EMPTY
SCHOOLROOM

THE ROOM WAS BARE except for about twenty-five desks with chairs. It was a big room and there were three large windows on the western wall. There was no blackboard. No teacher's desk. No charts or maps or pictures on the walls. Only twenty-five desks or so, with chairs.

And it was not enjoyable to Dr. Reuben to undergo these *reversals of roles*. Why had the conference organizers included this excursion on the program anyway? Here they were, perhaps twenty professional *academics* from universities all across the country, with Doctorates in linguistics, theory, history, sitting at little Hutterite schooldesks like *children*. And lecturing to them, standing in the front of the room, was a little Hutterite *girl*. What was she, seventeen? With a kerchief over the head. A dark flowery skirt and tennis shoes.

The fog was beginning to lift, she could see that. There were mornings when it was not possible to see anything outside her apartment window in Edmonton. It was a small flat with an outdated color scheme. These days all was supposed to be pale mauve and sea green, pink and pastel and copper like scoured roofs of new European buildings. Postmodernist architecture: it was beginning to grate on her how all new buildings and all renovations were in exactly the same style. Her place had a dark brown rug and her furniture was brown. Perhaps the cycle would return to brown some-day and then she would be in vogue again.

There were mornings when she felt closed in by the fog and she could not get up the stamina to dress, curl her hair, put a coat on and walk to her office. Fortu-nately all her classes this year were in the afternoon. She delayed going to work. Sometimes she felt hot and sweaty for no good reason, as if she had a fever, and her head felt full of wool. No matter how much coffee she drank, the sensation of being ill would not leave her.

Hour passed on hour. She knew she had to go. Students were waiting for her in front of her office. Their essays were folded up under their arms and they wanted to ask her what they did wrong. Show me what my mistakes are. Make me better. She tried to concentrate, wiped her forehead with a Kleenex. The sides of her nose were sweaty and she wiped them with the tips of her fingers. Professor Norwick from history came down to say hello. Her condition embarrassed her. She wished he would go away and come back another time, when she felt more normal. When she was more herself.

It was not easy to get things right: to maintain control. Dr. Reuben did not like losing control. She found it hard to keep up with her research. Doing so meant she had to take the long walk along the pretentiously named "Ho Chi Min Trail" to the library. A hundred students lined the walls, wasting time being silly. She had to walk around among the stacks, feeling clammy and hot. As she was closing in on the journal she was looking for she felt faint, suddenly, and went to the nearest chair. She wanted to run before the oppressive atmosphere of the library made her pass out.

She hated libraries because they made her sick. Physically ill. She hated museums for the same reason. And churches. Any place where you could not relax, have a soft drink, be yourself. These dry, sterile places. And here, this Hutterite schoolroom. They were going to be taken to the butchering room, the kitchen, the accounting room, the henhouse, the dairy. This would take at least two hours, if not more. She could not imagine how she would get through this tour.

The last time Norwick popped into her office she was in no condition to see him, or be seen by him. It was Monday. On Sunday, the day before, some young journalist had travelled on Via Rail clear across the prairies to do an interview with her for some third-rate publication. She had agreed to do it but the train was seven hours late. Instead of coming at three in the afternoon, he came at ten-thirty that night. They did the interview anyway and stayed up until two in the morning.

There was no sleep that night. To keep the journalist awake she made espresso coffee. Then she drank some herself. At six she finally got up after a wakeful few hours in bed and started a weary, blurry workday. By afternoon she had dark circles around her eyes. She was too tired to wash her hair and was convinced she looked a fright.

He had to come in that day. It was fated that he should see her at her worst. He appeared in the door in his dark blue trenchcoat and hat. He actually wore a Sherlock Holmes hat and always carried a briefcase. Norwick was married but that did not seem to matter these days. People were always leaving their spouses and joining up with others. It was endemic. He sat down across her desk with his devil-may-care smile waiting for her to say something funny.

It was just the emptiness of the room. Even though

most of the desks were now filled with people, the barrenness of these interiors made them seem empty. The Hutterite girl in her tennis shoes spoke in a high-pitched monotone. For every question the academics threw out at her, the response was the same. The girl let a brief moment pass while she stared emptily in the direction of the person asking the question. She did not look *at* you, just somehow *in your direction.*

They were asking how many pupils there were in the Colony. *Twenty-one.* How long did they receive an education. *Up to age fifteen.* What did they do at fifteen. *Take their place in the Colony.* What if a child wanted to learn more. *He would learn from elders in the Colony whatever practical skill he wanted to master.* Were they allowed to read books. *Yes.* Was there a library in the Colony. *No.* Then what did they read for pleasure. *The Bible.*

Dr. Reuben had a memory. It was something hidden in the recesses of her mind that came crawling out while she listened to her colleagues badger the young girl with questions. The girl was answering so obediently. When she herself was fifteen. It was the end of exams. An early spring day, perhaps May. The air was fresher than usual that time of year. She was waiting for a bus to take her to the city for the last time where she would see her parents again after a winter away at school. For some reason, she was not looking forward to moving back in with them.

There was a cool wind blowing so she went inside the schoolhouse. All the students were gone and the schoolhouse was empty. It was an old school. The yellow paint was peeling off the outside walls. The desks were old and carved up with pocketknives. The room smelled of old chalk and stagnant sweat. She went over to the window where she could see the bus coming down the hill in time to run out before it stopped in front of the building. She had half an hour to wait. She looked out at the empty hills, devoid of growth. The hillsides were naked. The glass in the window was grimy.

Sitting on one of the desks she pulled out her knapsack. In it there was a book she had found in the debris of a relative's library. She stole it, more or less stole it because it was about to be thrown away, and kept it hidden since. The book was in English. She had done very well in English, it was actually her best subject. The English teacher was pleased with her. She opened the book and began to read. A paperback. It was surprisingly easy reading.

As she sat there in silence preening at the pages with the miniature type, someone walked into the empty schoolroom. She looked up. It was her English teacher. "What are you doing here?" the teacher asked in surprise. "I'm waiting for a bus," she answered. Moving closer, the woman noticed she was reading. "And what are you reading?" the teacher asked with a pleasant smile. For a moment she wondered whether she should quickly close the book and put it in her knapsack without a word. Perhaps she should run out with the book hidden under her jacket. Perhaps she should simply show it. Just come out with it. Let the chips fall where they may.

She handed the bulky paperback to the teacher and said "It's a book in English." The teacher took it, still smiling, and looked at the cover. The picture showed a golden image of a mosque. The teacher's smile instantly left her face. The title. *The Glorious Koran.* The woman looked at her in disbelief. She did not say anything but obviously a million thoughts were racing through her head. She handed her back the book and said quietly, "Are you crazy?"

Are you crazy? Dr. Reuben had still not forgotten that question. Some things you may read, others you may not. Are you allowed to go to the library and borrow books in town? *Yes. But we do not have much free time.* Does anyone ever leave the Colony? *Sometimes. But it is very rare.* Do the women stay in the Colony after marriage? *No. They have to go to the Colony of their husbands.* Are you allowed to marry inside your Colony? *No. We are not allowed.*

Outside the window of the schoolroom a small
group of boys stood idly in a cluster. Perhaps there
were three or four of them, dressed in black pants with
suspenders, dark shirts and black caps. The pants of
these boys were always too short. When they appeared
in the city, at the farmers' market or in the grocery store
where they sometimes came in family groups, the pants
always ended well above the ankles. The boys had a
peculiar habit of keeping their hands in their pockets
constantly and leaning on one leg. They looked like
they were waiting for eternity. And it was to be a long
wait. They knew it was a long wait.

Dr. Reuben felt a nudge at her sleeve. She looked up
and saw everyone was leaving the schoolroom. Dr.
Dreiser was pulling her sleeve. "Are you coming?" he
said, half smiling. He knew she had a tendency to let
her mind wander if she was not entirely absorbed in
what was going on. At department meetings, he often
took a seat beside her just to keep her from melting
away. Those were his words. He accused her, affectionately, of "melting away." He was an elderly professor
of literature, now about to retire after over thirty years
of teaching and writing. He was so calm and fatherly.
Yes, *fatherly*.

The group filed out of the schoolroom, which dou-
bled as a church and sacristy. This room was where they
had their Sunday meetings, as well as their Colony

Council meetings and their prayer gatherings. When they stepped out of the building there was a mild wind blowing from the mountains. The Colony was just north of Calgary. The expanse of land in every direction was devoid of growth. It was hard to believe there were fields of rye and flax there in the summers. Perhaps there were none. Dr. Reuben was no longer sure. Except the lightly undulating prairie was grey and hard and uninviting.

They followed the Hutterite girl who walked briskly ahead of them into the dairy. What seemed like a hundred cows were boxed up in shining clean stalls and attached to their udders were milking gadgets that led the milk into sterilized milk jugs off in another cubicle room. A small glass encasement at the side contained a computer. The computer registered exactly how much each cow ate and how much milk was coming, and regulated intake and output to a fine point. One man in the Colony knew how to operate the computer.

The Polish professor from Montréal was shaking his head in disbelief at the back of the group. Dr. Reuben did not know his name, but he seemed to her a devious sort, slightly hunched over and forever with a critical smile scowling on his face. He spoke with a heavy accent. Leaning over towards Dr. Reuben he said, "Fake. This is a fake farm. Not real." "What do you mean by that?" Dr. Reuben asked under her breath while pretending to listen to the explanation about milking procedures from the girl. "It's too sterile," said the Polish professor. "Too mechanical. Too much technology."

Dr. Reuben did not think the comment was worth an answer. She used to go to the cow barn when she was young to fetch milk for her family. It was a short walk and Avie, the man who owned the large stretch of land that led to the river, owned a few cows that he milked every day. She brought a bucket and he milked them by hand, pulling until the milk spurted out. There was heavy cream on the top. They had a special pudding they made out of the first milk taken after a cow had calved. She hated the taste. She spit it out into her bowl again and everyone at the table made noises of disgust.

He did it twice. Not just once. Norwick appeared another time at her office door on one of her *bad* days. She was up the night before grading papers until three in the morning. She was too tired to think about what clothes she was wearing and went to work in a black cotton skirt and grey sweater that were anything but elegant. Her complexion must have been pale, her face haggard. He walked in, since she had forgotten to close her office door, looking fresh as ever. How did he manage to *control* everything the way he did? How did he do it? And why did she always feel so *unclean*? That was it. She felt somehow *disgusting*.

She wanted to get to the bottom of that feeling. Find out where it came from, who convinced her that she was disgusting. In her academic years she managed to *intellectualize* the phenomenon, to talk about it objectively, to think about it as if it were someone else's problem. But it was still not possible to get rid of the *feeling*. Norwick wanted her to come for coffee in the medical building. His wife, he said, was just about ready for a break and they should join her. Dr. Reuben did not want to say no. They were her friends.

She put on her boots and coat and they walked across campus to the medical sciences laboratories. He took the elevator every time, never used the stairs. Perhaps this way he avoided breaking out into a sweat? Dr. Reuben herself always took the stairs. She arrived at her office perspiring from the long climb. They stepped out of the elevator and she followed Norwick down a small maze of hallways. How *sterile*, she thought: everything was so clean and whitewashed.

They found Norwick's wife in the x-ray lab setting up a machine. She must have come from another world. It never failed. Dr. Reuben looked at her with a sense of *intimidation*. There was never a crease in her clothes, never a tired wrinkle on her face, never an uncertain moment about her. She must have come from another world. What kind of fortunate background was it she had? She wore heels, dark green slacks and a soft blouse with shoulder pads. When she went out with her husband she dressed in shining white dancing dresses and her hair sparkled darkly.

Norwick's wife had to finish x-raying a mannequin head. Dr. Reuben and Norwick waited outside the room and looked in through a large window meant for students to observe the instructor's x-raying techniques without being exposed to the rays. In the dentist's chair a head was perched quite by itself, the mouth stretched open on one side and the x-ray gun pointing at the left cheek. It was a brown head, perhaps rubber or plastic, with no traces of hair. It was an absolutely practical head with no aesthetic features. Dr. Reuben felt hot in her warm coat. She was aware of a sense of discomfort in the presence of the disembodied head: as if that imitation of a human part had something she did not. Something *more preferable than she, with all her human failings and bodily distractions.* And the knowledge that she could never become *pure intellect.*

It was cultural. It must be cultural, Dr. Reuben assured herself. There must be something she herself had *inherited* that prevented her from feeling *clean* like Norwick's wife. Even now, in her forties and educated out of all that, Dr. Reuben could not get over the sense that at certain times of the month she must not even *look* at a man. She went about her business with her eyes lowered. She did not look a man in the face, but somehow only *in his direction*. She felt *embarrassed* by herself, her body. She felt *humiliated* by her physicality. Sometimes she *wanted* to cover herself from head to toe in heavy dark robes and hide her face *behind a veil*.

No. It was absurd. The group had been through the henhouse where all the hens were boxed up in little tiny cubicles with slides underneath for the eggs to roll down through into the boxes. It was mechanical but efficient. All the surfaces were stainless steel, wiped clean so meticulously not a single speck was left behind. She could see the scrapes on the surfaces where the scouring brush had been. Where did all this energy to clean come from? This desire to *overclean*?

They were marched into the Colony kitchen. There eleven women, all wearing ankle-length skirts, aprons, dark cotton blouses and kerchiefs over their heads hiding their hair, were making cheese sandwiches. The bread they used was white and soft, perfect in texture and shape. The cheese was cleanly cut and the sandwiches were arranged on stainless steel trays in patterns that were never broken. The trays were carried into the dining room where all the Colony members ate together. The older ones first, the younger ones later. There were no pictures on the whitewashed walls. Nothing but six very long tables with wooden chairs all around.

Dr. Reuben stood with the others observing the

women make sandwiches at the kitchen table. One woman glanced at her. Like the others, she had no expression on her face and her look was unfocussed. But Dr. Reuben felt she was being observed furtively. She remembered that the coat she was wearing had not been to the cleaners in four years. *Four years.* The kitchen with its gleaming surfaces and its absence of any odor, suddenly felt *oppressive.*

Dr. Reuben left the kitchen alone while the others were still getting an explanation of the kneading machine in the bakery. It was a huge machine consisting of an enormous bowl and a gigantic kneading device that went around and around in the bowl. Exactly so many revolutions for exactly so many loaves of bread. When she came out, the cluster of boys had moved over to the kitchen. They stood idly against the wall and looked at her without interest but apparently curious. Out in the open spaces she realized that this Colony had *no place to hide.* Every move was observable.

At the kitchen window a heavy man stood looking out. He was large: tall and fat, his belly protruded imposingly. He stood keeping some kind of watch over the women working in the kitchen. Perhaps he was not keeping watch. He could just be waiting for food. But he looked out the window with a *proprietary* air. Dr. Reuben noticed him standing there. He was inside the kitchen and she was the only one outside. What would it be like to live here and be a Hutterite? she wondered. To have that large red-bearded man in black slacks with suspenders looking over her shoulder? To be always clean? To be just like everyone else: the same thin face, the same pale blue eyes?

No, she mustn't do this. Dr. Reuben reprimanded herself almost instinctively. There was a boundary problem, she knew that. She had been told she was *boundariless*. She had a way of *melting in*. Of always imagining herself *in someone else's shoes*. She imagined what it would be like to be Norwick's wife. Was it an uncomplicated life? Did he *accept her* on her worst days? She had heard there was a place in the world where people bathed together, men and women, in outdoor hot water pools. There was snow on the ground and frost in the air, but people *threw off their clothes and went into the hot water* as if it were midsummer. It might be night: the stars were shining and steam from the natural hot water rose into the darkness. People bathed and bathed, laughing, singing, free.

There was a place like that, wasn't there? She walked over to the school building again where the tour had started. The black clad boys followed her mistrustfully with their unfocussed eyes. She no longer wanted to be part of the program. She could feel the thin wind playing in the air. She entered the empty schoolroom and sat down. There was no sound. Suddenly a man appeared in the door. He came over to her and sat down beside her. It was Dr. Dreiser. He put his comfortable hand on her shoulder. "Are you all right my dear?" he asked softly. "I saw you leave and walk over here."

Dr. Reuben did not answer. She was afraid she would burst into tears, inexplicably. Battling her barely controllable feelings, she put her hand on Dr. Dreiser's in a gesture of gratefulness. What was it they said about him: Dr. Dreiser? "He is everybody's favorite uncle," that was it. Someone had said that and she no longer remembered who. How nice that he *accepted her*. With all her flaws, all the many mistakes she made. Her inability to *get things right* as though she did not belong in this world. They sat together for a while, her hand covering his, resting on her shoulder.

SORROW COW

Her name was *Sorrow Cow*. I had barely time to wonder about the names of the animals because R.D. and Danielle were already in their boots and jackets and thick scarves around their necks waiting for me to come outside. It must have been minus thirty-five, at least. December in Alberta. Christmas, as a matter of fact, and I had time to see the pastures and animals before I was to come back and help Danielle's mother stuff the turkey and grandmother mash the potatoes. The potatoes were my affair, we knew that, but grandmother had to feel productive. I had my boots on and followed the two young people outside. This was where Danielle grew up. "This is where we used to make a path to the skating rink," Danielle yelled back to me. The two of them were already way ahead of me, running clumsily in their winter gear. The expedition we were on concerned the business of introducing me to the farm animals. Danielle was now living in the city with R.D., my son that is, who had discovered her in a philosophy class at the university and now they appeared inseparable. So much the better, I always thought. Love stabilizes and matures people.

I was in for the holidays from the Okanagan Valley. Mostly to see R.D. and Danielle, but also to see what Christmas on the Alberta farm was like. They were at the horse pasture already, waiting for me at the gate. The wind was still now and the snow was knee deep and getting crusty from the cold. Beside the horse field was the cow pasture, only I could see no cows. "They all cower over by the feeding bin," Danielle was calling. When I caught up to them they were singling out the cows. "That one," the girl told me pointing to a medium-sized cow standing still by the feed as though lost in thought, "that one is *Sorrow Cow*." "What kind of a name for a cow is that?" I asked, genuinely curious. Danielle laughed her hilarious laugh, throwing her dark head back and opening her mouth in pure joy. "R.D. named her," she asserted. "It's just," R.D. broke in to explain matter-of-factly, "Danielle's dad took her little calf away one day and sold it in the city and she was crying all night, once when we were here for the

weekend, so I named her _Sorrow Cow_." "Oh yeah!"
Danielle added, "oh yeah, and tell her how you sat on the
fence there and sang Frank Sinatra songs for Sorrow
Cow for _four hours_!" And she was still laughing. "I sat
on the fence right there and sang Frank Sinatra songs
for her for a few hours," he said. "She liked it." "She
liked it?" I repeated questioningly, trying to figure the
level of sarcasm involved. "Loved it!" Danielle said,
leaning over rapturously as if the final blow had come
to the hilarity. "She loved it! She stood there like stone
and he was sitting on the fence singing Frank Sinatra,
the whole album!" "Yeah," R.D. giggled lightly along,
"do do do, all of me why not take all of me."

And they were running down the path along the
fence where Danielle's dad took the feed no doubt
twice a day or some such thing. For the horses and the
cows. It wasn't a big operation, only a small herd of
cattle, and I knew he was recently in town to buy a bull.
He sells a calf for — what was it he said he got for a
calf, was it five hundred? Or was that too much? I
figured in my head briefly and quickly what one would
have to do to make a living at a small farm like this as
I followed along the fence. The two young ones were
already climbing over farther down. I climbed over the
fence after them and caught up with them at the hay
pile where the cows were standing. The cows appeared
unconcerned about us. R.D. went from one to the

other saluting them and saying things. Sorrow Cow, the only one I knew by name so far, gave me a look, hay sticking clumsily out of the corner of her mouth. "Can't you see I'm no good without you," R.D. was continuing his humming and Danielle was urging us on excitedly. "You have to see where we used to go skating," she pushed, "Susan and I, the little lake dad always cleared in the winter." And she was gone down the pasture. R.D. took his time, stopping to greet the horses as well. "How do I express my affection for them?" he called to Danielle across the snow and she was already sitting on the fence on the other side, waiting and laughing.

I caught up with her and waited with her before trekking through the woods to get to the lake. We were located a few hundred miles north of Edmonton, but I never really counted the distance. It was an overcast day, that Christmas Day, and everybody was back at the house. "Is he going to sing for the horses?" Danielle gasped. No, I didn't think so, but he was trying to make some sort of contact. "This may take him a while," I suggested. So Danielle and I headed off through the forest. The snow was deeper in the woods. Tall evergreen Alberta pines stood over us, towering half skeptically. Silence had spread into the woods like a fog. "Look at that!" Danielle broke the quiet. I turned to the horse pasture where she was looking. Sure enough,

R.D. was walking across the field and behind him the horses had decided to follow in single formation. Somehow he had acquired their trust. How did he do that? It was an amazing feat. "That's it!" I heard Danielle call out. We had reached the lake. It was no bigger than, say, half an acre, but obviously quite useful. "We used to have great hockey games here, Susan and dad and I, when we were little," Danielle explained.

Then she was running onto the ice and R.D. after. Before I knew it they were way on the other side, sliding in their boots, catching each other, pushing each other, laughing, yelling something. I took a spin on my boots as well but soon I was taken by the silence of the Alberta prairie and the two slender brown-haired young people enjoying life, and it was Christmas and all the trees seemed to be decked in white ribbons. But I had promised to come back to the kitchen to help stuff the turkey. I signalled to them that I was turning around and left them cascading across the ice and went into the forest again. For a short while I didn't know which direction was which. Once in the forest it felt like no human habitation could be anywhere near. I imagined myself getting lost, wandering always farther north. North without end. Quickly I rehearsed what I knew of survival techniques: build a lean-to fire. A reflector fire can keep you in seventy degrees temperature even though it is minus sixty.

Scrape the bark off the trees and eat the larva. Are there larva at this time of year? Signal for help. And so on. I was half lost in dream, not really concerned. Thinking how odd it was after all that the boy I raised on buses and airplanes and ships had found roots on an Alberta farm and was talking to the animals.

Eventually I came to the small herd of cows at the feeding spot. The cows still stood there eating. I wondered how cold it had to get before they became uncomfortable, and remembered Danielle's dad assuring me they could stay outside all winter, even here in northern Alberta. I stopped at the herd and felt the warmth of the animals around me. They paid very little attention to my presence. Behind me, somewhere in the woods, my son was passing into a new life with which I had so little familiarity. And that talking to the animals. I suppose it had to come from somewhere. Sorrow Cow was still in the same spot. I walked up to her and looked at her hang-dog eyes, large and wet. Quite inappropriately I recalled that movie with Buster Keaton where he falls in love with a cow in the field because of her deep brown eyes and then does all kinds of things to prevent her from ending up in the slaughterhouse. Chicago, it was, and I laughed so hard in the movie theater I could hardly stand it. I remember that herd of cows blocking the traffic of Chicago and Buster Keaton jumping from one railway car to another. I patted Sorrow Cow on the head between the ears, and she looked at me tiredly. "Somehow," I found myself saying, "one way or another, the likes of us, our little ones," I assured her, "one way or another, we lose them." She appeared to understand me, only for a moment because I knew, of course, she really didn't. Although who could say. "Nothing is for certain," I said out loud. "Only one thing, we lose them." But I was already on my way back to the fence and I climbed it and saw the house in the distance. Heading back up the path I gave the cow a last glance, and she was still looking at me even while she was chewing. And just to remind her of the connection, just in case she didn't know where I came from all of a sudden that Christmas day, I hummed ever so softly over the fence the song she surely recognized by now, "All of me why not take all of me can't you see I'm no good without you," and I guessed she was listening because I think she was. And from the path I could see Danielle's mother and grand-mother measuring out spices and bread crumbs at the kitchen counter through the window. The hard snow crunched. "Don't we," I added as I turned to the house, "don't we *Sorrow Cow*?"

THE GREEN DRESS

IN DEFIANCE OF EVERYTHING, Miranda bought a
green dress. The purchase was an act of defiance
because this was not an ordinary green dress. It was
floor-length nylon, shining green and it spread out
around her like a pool of the purest, deepest spring
water as it shimmered in the sun. The shoulders were
bare but on the tips of the top of her arms the black
nylon swept around in giant ribbon-like fashion, en-
casing her neck and head in a frame of dark shining
shadows that resembled the night sky filtered through
with Northern Lights.

Or so it seemed to Miranda. She was six thousand
dollars in debt and the dress cost seven hundred and
eighty-two dollars, but one thousand more or less did
not seem to her to matter. There was also the question

of practicality. The dress was meant for an extremely formal occasion — an Embassy Ball or dinner with the Prime Minister or the Order of Canada Award Ceremonies, for example. But Miranda was not expecting any such occasion in the next few months. She had nothing on her agenda, in fact. *Nothing.*

Perhaps the very absence of *formality* in her life made her want the dress so much. The *ordinariness* of her existence. She was miserable these days. Work was becoming extremely boring. She went to the office where she was secretary to a company whose directors never showed their faces. All her assignments came over the phone or via computer. She went there every morning promptly at nine, got her habitual Styrofoam cup of coffee from "Cookies by George," sat down in her swivel chair and looked at the pile of correspondence for her to answer. Every day she worked her way through that stack of mail, typing on the computer everything she was supposed to type out, and every night she closed the "IN" file knowing that next morning it would be there again as if she had never touched it. Only it would be a new pile of mail. She began to see that the more mail she answered for her firm, the more mail came in. It was a vicious cycle which her bosses wanted to perpetuate. Mail was money. The money was for them, the work was for her: always more of it.

Miranda earned exactly one thousand two hundred thirty-four dollars and sixty-three cents a month, take home. Of that sum, five hundred went to rent and two hundred for utilities. That left about five hundred dollars to buy food, cosmetics, clothes, soap, shoes, and gas for every month. And to do the laundry, which cost her two-fifty per load, pay for parking, which cost her twenty dollars a month, and go to movies, which now cost seven dollars a shot. In order not to go out she bought Cable television, but that was another twenty-four dollars a month. The opera was out of the question, for the cheapest tickets were forty-two dollars, on the third balcony in the extreme right-hand wing on Monday night. Although she did so want to see *La Bohème*, where the tubercular woman dies in the arms of her beloved in the artists' garret over the roofs of . . . Vienna? Firenze? And they sang such beautiful solos of love and passion and tragic fate. For all these reasons Miranda made heavy use of her Visa card and was now six thousand seven hundred and eighty-two dollars in debt.

It was the middle of winter. January. And the darkest time of the year. Up in the most northerly city of the Canadian provinces, excluding the Northwest Territories, it was impossible not to notice how dawn arrived later and later every morning and dusk crept in earlier every evening. Now when she went to work it was still dark and when she came home again it was dark. The daylight hours she spent cooped up on the fourth floor of a downtown office building that had strung yellow lights over its entire thirty-two floors to give the illusion of a Christmas tree to airplanes passing overhead bound for the Municipal airport.

At home Miranda had a cat she called Bugsy Malone, an electric coffee-maker, a television, a VCR, and an oversized photograph of two European lovers saying "au revoir." She did not have a toaster or a microwave oven, but those were purchases she intended to make in the future. She had a small personal library of bestsellers she found at Shoppers' Drug Mart and Safeway and a few picture books from Aspen Books. The best part of her "holdings," as she was fond of putting it, was her wardrobe. Her *trousseau*. She had in her closet some of the nicest dresses and suits that could be found. And scores of shoes.

It was the clothes that cost so much. She would not be in debt to that degree if she did not buy clothes. But it was a weakness and she was convinced one had to indulge at least *one* weakness in order to stay happy. Although she was trying to *cut down*. Her friend Stella was cutting down on smoking, which seemed just as hard as *not to shop*. But the aggravation for Miranda was that as she tried to stay away from boutiques with lovely fashions for women, there were always more and more of them appearing. And their stock was always more and more interesting. To top it off there was the ever-present *West Edmonton Mall*, which was the largest shopping mall in the world, guaranteeing that no one needed to go to Paris or London or New York or even Toronto *ever again*. Everything could be had *right here*.

During the week Miranda came home from work every day at five-fifteen, hung up her dress carefully and put it in the closet if it could be worn once again, or in the doorway if it needed a wash. She tied up her hair and took a shower, soaping off her whole body the dust of paper ripping off the printer for eight hours. She put a TV dinner in the oven, nowadays usually it was "Light Tonight," and she and Bugsy Malone, for whom she opened a tin of Cat Chow, had dinner. After washing the plate, she and Bugsy sat down to watch a movie. These days there was a rerun of the classics, many of them with Audrey Hepburn and William Holden, and she enjoyed them immensely. As Bugsy crept around in a constant attempt at finding the optimal resting position that would include some part of his owner's body, Miranda sat riveted to the screen.

Weekends were more difficult to get through. Miranda had read in one of the women's magazines she occasionally picked off the racks when doing her grocery shopping that some people suffer from *weekenditis*. That was a fear of weekends. For some it was intolerable to think that stores closed, post offices closed, and it was not necessary to go to work. As a result people were thrown *on their own devices*. Some had no "devices" to resort to and needed the routine of the workday to make sense of things. After considerable reflection, Miranda was convinced she had a touch of weekenditis. Nothing serious, just a tinge of it.

To get through the weekends, Miranda had therefore devised a routine which she called "the plan." On Saturday mornings she bought croissants for breakfast at the cornerstore that had a little bakery in the back and opened at nine a.m. After munching on those, she cleaned house and washed clothes until noon. Then she took a walk along the river, knowing it was necessary to make a space for fresh air sometime during the week. After her walk she got in her car, which was a blue Firefly because that was the cheapest new car she could buy, and drove to the West Edmonton Mall, where she sauntered, lingered and lounged around, looking at clothes, pictures, goldfish and children skating, for the afternoon. Sometimes she was not home from her Mall excursion until seven, and Bugsy was waiting, hungry and impatient, meowing in long drawls with a full throat.

It was on a Saturday in the middle of January that Miranda drove into the Mall parking lot, parked to the right of her usual stall, which someone had taken, and walked in through the east entrance number thirty-eight. She saw it was not very crowded today, which made her glad. The Mall could be a hassle if too many people were about, which happened sometimes — like early December. She took her usual walk through Eaton's hat department where she saw a bowler hat as a fashion item hanging on the hatrack. She took it down, put it on her head and looked in the mirror. It was a wonderful hat and it cost only twelve dollars and ninety-five cents. She bought it, telling the sales woman "It's my day to have fun," and walked out of the store with the hat on.

Sauntering down the hallways, Miranda window-shopped in her bowler hat for the better part of half an hour. There were new spring fashions beginning to appear in the windows and she studied the seasonal color scheme. Some fashion designers in Paris or New York probably sat down in a boardroom in the penthouse of some Manhattan office building and decided on the seasonal changes to be made that would make last summer's wardrobe obsolete and require a brand new shopping spree for every appearance-conscious woman. "This spring we will highlight the oranges and pale colors, so that last summer's bright colors will be too gaudy," one designer would declare, and the rules would be laid down.

But Miranda did not mind. In fact, she enjoyed being

forced to replenish her wardrobe every season. New fashions gave her a reason for buying new clothes, a *justification* for her weekly shopping days. She went up the escalator to the second floor, which was really a mezzanine, overlooking the first floor. She enjoyed the mezzanine more, for it was quieter and the stores were more elegant. All the expensive clothiers were located there and the best jewellers. She stopped to look at diamonds encased in glass and rubies perched on gold rings under the transparent counters. At an accessories store she tried on costume earrings and since they were only eleven forty-nine she bought a pair of green ones that covered half her cheek when she had them on, for they were nice and large.

With her green costume earrings and bowler hat on, Miranda was wandering from store to store when she saw the green dress. It was not in a window but was hanging for display in the middle of the floor as you entered. The store was a formal-wear place called "Mirabella's," and there were only glitzy cocktail and dance dresses for sale there. A mannequin bodice held the dress up and the shining green nylon glittered in the bright lights and mirrors all around the room. It was a wonderful dress: so very formal, absolutely elegant, and nothing gauche about it. No baubles or cheap tinselly buttons to make it shine. Just pure and simple nylon, without decorations, that flowed from the waist all around.

A short-haired Chinese woman came up and asked if she could help. She was an impeccably dressed sales clerk with extremely tasteful make-up and a skirt and blouse that were unobtrusive but fine. Miranda hesitated a moment and then said "Could I try this dress on, size seven?" Beaming with a smile, the sales clerk led her to a rack where two other such dresses were hanging, but they were bright red. Eventually she removed the green one from the display mannequin and hung it in a dressing room with a full-length mirror. Miranda followed, closed the door, and changed into the ballroom gown.

That day Miranda was wearing old jeans, a winter sweater and high snow boots with thick socks underneath. It was not the proper attire to try formal gowns in. She had also neglected to curl her hair and was looking quite plain once the bowler hat was removed and the earrings were off. But she took them all off anyway, borrowed a pair of high heels from the store which they kept around for customers like her, and slipped on the green dress. Underneath it she had nothing but a pair of bikini panties. She zippered the bodice up at the back and adjusted the black shoulders that were designed to drape across the upper arm instead of the shoulder itself. Then she turned to look at herself in the mirror.

By some miracle of the senses, some shifting of

reality, some magic wand of perspective, Miranda found she had been transformed into the most beautiful Cinderella at the ball or Snow White after the kiss of the prince. Was it an optical illusion? She was no longer plain. Her brown hair flowed in copper strands about her oval face and onto her bare shoulders. Her brown eyes shone with the reflection of the dress. Her arms, which hung bare at her side, were no longer pale but glowed with a golden luminosity she could not account for. Her full lips were suddenly dark red and shining, even without lipstick. The dress itself fit her perfectly and sat snug at the waist and covered her breasts just enough to give her the appearance of nudity under the shimmering fabric.

Miranda opened the door to the dressing room and went into the main store where there were enormous three-way mirrors to see herself from all sides. The lighting was different out there and perhaps she would have a more *realistic* view of what she looked like. She went to the largest mirrors near the front of the store where some of the lighting from the hall would filter in and take away the designed lighting of the store. The sales clerk followed her and together they examined the dress. But it was not an illusion put on by some clever dressing-room designer. Even out here, where the light was not half as deliberate, Miranda was astounded to see herself so beautiful. So *incredibly beautiful*. It was almost impossible to believe.

Miranda stood in front of these mirrors for a good while. She said nothing but simply stared at her reflection in wonder and surprise. She could neither smile nor make a comment to the clerk, who was giving directions to another customer just then anyway. As Miranda stood there, she realized someone out in the hall was also standing still, looking at her. She turned her head slightly to see. It was a tall and slender man wearing a dark grey knee-length coat and grey slacks and his hair was black with an occasional strand of white. He was definitely looking at her, unapologetically. She turned all the way to face him so he could see she did not appreciate being observed. Then she saw who it was. Goodness. Good night! *It was Mr. Kim!*

Mr. Kim was none other than the director of the Foreign Exchange Bank on a Hundred and First Street where she went every day at three-ten with the company's cheques for deposit from markets in South Korea. Mr. Kim had taken the firm's account on personally, so when she came in she dealt with him directly. That was because he had special connections with a bank in Seoul which handled the transactions with her firm. They usually went into one of the small offices at the back, not the director's office, and Mr. Kim filled in the deposit books for her and handed them back. He was very quiet and said little, but sometimes his face had a certain *expression*. It was not meant to convey anything special, just a kind of *appreciation*. The appreciation, Miranda was beginning to notice, was not really about the bank having a good client in the company she worked for, as she had once thought. That expression, the slight smile he could give without actually smiling, was meant for her. *For her personally*.

Once Miranda had determined the nature of Mr. Kim's attitude to her, she began to look him over more carefully. It was undeniable, she had to admit it, that Mr. Kim was a handsome man. *Probably the handsomest man in Edmonton*. He did not look *Korean*, really, like he was supposed to. He was very tall and his bones were large but well proportioned. He was slender and without his jacket and with his sleeves rolled up, Miranda noticed long strands of sinews that went up his arms under his golden skin. They were the *sexiest* arms she had ever seen in a man. Once she was bold enough to ask him whether he was from Korea. He looked up at her, smiled slightly and nodded. That was all. "South Korea?" Miranda added to her question. Mr. Kim did not look up but continued filling in the account book. "Yes," he answered a little absently, "but my family was originally from the North."

That brief conversation constituted the full extent

of what she knew about Mr. Kim. But Miranda decided to *add* to her information by going to the library and reading about Korea and why some families moved from the North to the South and why some Koreans looked so *different*. As if they belonged to no place at all, no discernible, known place on the globe. Why, in short, some of them might look like Mr. Kim, so inexplicably good looking and so casually *perfect* somehow.

What she learned by reading infused Miranda's *interest* in Mr. Kim with a great deal of *romance* and *drama*. Korea, it turned out, was a divided country, which she already knew. But the border was completely closed. North Koreans in the South had *fled* as refugees before the border was closed off. They were running away from Russians who invaded Korea from the north at the end of World War II. Late in the nineteenth century Russia had had trading influence in Korea. As a result of this early trading and of Russia's invasion of Korea in 1945, there was traffic between the Caucasians of Russia and the Orientals of Korea. The encounters between the two races were invariably *unpleasant* and sometimes *violent*. She read of Korean women hiding out in the mountains from roughneck Russian traders and soldiers. If Mr. Kim was not one of these *impure* Koreans that existed because of such unfortunate unions, then, Miranda had decided, he was some kind of Tatar. A Tatar, explained her *Webster's New World Dictionary*, is "a member of any of the East Asiatic tribes who invaded West Asia and Eastern Europe in the Middle Ages."

Mr. Kim was not exactly facing Miranda, and it appeared he had stopped while walking and had not bothered to turn around, not exactly intending to stop. But Miranda could see in his half-smiling face, for he was *actually smiling*, that expression of *warm appreciation*. She stood transfixed in place, frozen in the middle of the floor before the great mirrors, unable to say a word or to turn away. And Mr. Kim could not be more than five feet away from her, standing in the doorway of "Mirabella's" apparently similarly frozen, not having intended to stop. But he took a step in Miranda's direction looking down at her as if observing from a great distance. He said to Miranda in a gentle but firm voice "This is very much like a traditional Korean dress." Then he nodded very slightly with his head in lieu of "goodbye" and continued on his way, disappearing behind the wall.

Miranda stood stock-still for a while, not exactly realizing Mr. Kim had gone. When she did, she turned towards the dressing room and ran as fast as the oceans of green nylon and borrowed high-heeled shoes three sizes too large for her feet would allow. When she got to her changing room, she slammed the door, locked it shut and pressed her forehead against the wall. The bodice of the new dress was suddenly too tight and her face was flushed. Should she be embarrassed? Was this embarrassing? She could not tell what Mr. Kim might think of a woman who tries on ballroom gowns in the middle of the day in January for no good reason. She hurriedly undressed, put her old jeans on again, her boots, coat, earrings and bowler hat and grabbed the green dress. At the counter the sales clerk made the transaction with Miranda's credit card that would enable her to take the dress home, wrapped the dress in a plastic bag, and Miranda made her way as fast as she could out to her Firefly and home.

When she got home it was earlier than usual on Saturdays. Bugsy Malone appeared surprised, having some second sense of time under his fur. Miranda kept her cat because Miss Golightly in *Breakfast at Tiffany's* had a cat that was orange like Bugsy. She took out a four-dollar can of Swedish sardines and opened it for the cat. No doubt Bugsy should have something out-of-the-ordinary too. She picked the cat up by his forelegs and the rest of his body dangled in midair. His shoulders were scrunched up under the pressure of Miranda's grip. She shook the cat once playfully and whispered to the completely limp animal "Do you suppose Mr. Kim would ever be so kind as to give us a reason for wearing our green dress, Bugsy?"

She put the cat down and he attacked the sardines with delight and admiration for his owner. Alternately licking the outside of the little fish, Bugsy looked up at Miranda with excessive affection and purrs. Miranda sat down on the floor to watch Bugsy Malone gorge himself. "Let's face it Bugsy," she confided to the cat as she took off her new earrings, one by one, and looked at them. "We're Fantasyland junkies, you and I. Aren't we?" Bugsy looked up once again in what seemed to be assent and meowed slightly. Miranda repeated herself. *"Shopping-mall junkies, aren't we."*

MASS AND A DANCE

THE GROUND CRACKLED WHEN she walked. It was frozen snow, not ice. Minus thirty-three. Smoke from all the chimneys filled the town of St. Norbert. The air was white. The sky was white. The sun was white. She had learned to like this place from constant use. The cornerstore, the little post office, the crude statue of Mother Mary across from the Catholic church. All the dedications in this tiny French Manitoba village to the battles of the Métis. History invaded by Winnipeg suburban developments: brand new single-storey homes erected in droves over the summer. When the wind blew, whole walls of the unfinished constructions collapsed. It was not a pretty village but it had that edge of ruined history about it. An old village cradled by the bend in the Red River that insinuated: you may have lost but you're still here.

That's the whole point right there, she thought to herself as she walked along the suburban street on her way home. To be *still here*. The thought stung her. She was placid enough yet maddened by a sense of inescapable grief: a grief that was like the atmosphere of the earth. Something so fundamental you know you cannot come out of it. A grief that comes to people when they know something that had life in it is irretrievably lost. It was not a person: it was a history. Is this how Native Indians feel, she asked herself, when they have lost territories to encroaching modernity? Or people who have lived in tiny railroad hamlets out on the prairies, when the railroad cuts service to them and the hamlet dies for lack of use? Do they feel like this?

She came to Canada because it was somehow no longer feasible to live in the town she came from. It was territory now laid waste. Since she could not stay there, she decided to quit the country altogether, refusing the daily reminders of loss: the cold rain, the northern wind, the midnight sun. She grew up in the Vestfirdir of Iceland, a desolate region far in the northwest of a desolate island in the North Atlantic. Life was never easy there, but when modernity invaded the island, new urban centers sucked people out of little hard-won villages and emptied them. She thought of modern civilization as a great sewer: a trashcan into which everything gets thrown.

What is still called Sléttuhreppur — "Plains District" — was once the northernmost inhabited region of the Vestfirdings. In nineteen-forty nearly five hundred people lived there. Ten years later it was a ghost fjord. The sun rose over Hornbjarg, illuminating the water in the bay, and no one saw. The church in Stadur was a ghost church. Small, wooden, white, four windows on each side and a tiny bell tower facing the sea. No one rang the bell. The Vestfirdings were gone.

She looked around her in the St. Norbert winter. It was so silent, she seemed to have lost her hearing. All she could see were bi-level houses squarely facing the sun. The crunchy sound of her footsteps seemed to come from inside a tunnel. A bird screeched. When she looked, there were only barren branches and the bird was gone.

She still did not know why all the Vestfirdings deserted Sléttuhreppur. Most of them went to the capital city in the south. Some went abroad: Greece, America, Spain. When they were gone, thinking they had improved their lot in life, they discovered they missed their northern Arctic environment. Services were cut so there was little hope of reestablishing a community. Instead they staged a *reunion*. The previous summer. She had come along with all the others. There would be a mass in the church and a dance in the schoolhouse. There was a chartered coach to Stadur in Adalvík and on the way they picked up Jakob, the priest from Ísafjördur, to bless them at the end of the weekend.

The last time she had been in the little church was at her confirmation. They were several very young angels draped in white from neck to toe. They made a holy procession down the isle, their black Psalters clutched to their chests. They knelt before the altar, hands folded, looking up. The priest placed his hand on her head. Her elaborate hairdo went down. She forgot about the blessing: her only thought was that the priest did not understand the matter of hairdos.

On Advent Sunday they always lit the candles and then they were angels holding candles. Hákon the composer brought a choir to sing for them. They sang a choral work he had composed: *The Gravestone Suite*. Hákon had gone to the graveyard and written chants of the inscriptions on all the tombstones. When he conducted this choir, he stood on a table so they could all see him. After Advent mass there was coffee in the community room. Hákon again got up on the table. He stood among the coffee cups and the choir sang a chant for the food.

For the reunion mass in Stadur, all the old relics were brought back and put in their former places. There must have been eighty people. No one could

bring the organ on the coach, so Reynir the organist
played the accordion instead. In the evening, Reynir
the organist played his accordion for the dance.

At the dance many women wore the national costume. Black skirts, black vests, white aprons and black
caps with long tassels. By midnight they were all tipsy.
By two in the morning these black swans all had to be
taken to the coach. They were smiling obliviously. She
had left the dance at seven next morning. Dawn had
long passed. The coach driver was waiting. Passengers
were impatient. Some were draped over their seats,
others curled into balls. An elderly Sléttuhreppur
farmer had imprisoned her in conversation in the
community kitchen, on the topic of education. Everyone thought they were doing something else. When
she came out and realized the communal mistake, she
was too embarrassed to correct it.

She crawled into her coach seat and went to sleep.
The elderly farmer's son, whom she had a crush on as
a teenager, had disappeared. He had long, dark blond
locks and an athletic body. She used to frequent socccr
matches just to look at his body. She went to men's
swimming competitions for the same reason. He had
not shown up for the reunion: they said he was somewhere in South Africa. After gymnasium in the city he
went to college in America where he met an education
student from South Africa, married her and went into

the South African bush while she did research on the education of native tribes.

Meanwhile she found herself in the dead of winter in the Canadian prairie. Manitoba. Stalled cars with their hoods up littered the highway in this cold. They stood abandoned, collecting a coating of ice. Schoolchildren rolled like balls out of the yellow schoolbus and trundled home, packed in snowsuits, scarves and moon boots. They had trouble walking straight bundled up as they were.

She wondered whether her *bitterness*, that must be the word, over the *dissolution* of her birth community had something to do with the young farmer's son who had seemed to her the ideal of northern beauty. That they were *forced* to part company: forced to be the captives of *distance*?

There were moments when she appreciated the scattered clouds as they conspired with the frost to block out the sun. Every cloud over the prairie had a southeastern lining, in gold. On days like this, all seemed to her discontinuity. No single train of thought remained steady. Stories were broken into flakes: of memory, of history, of ice. Sometimes it snowed. She had never been able to relate a story from beginning to end in this place. Not even to herself. Yet life seemed to fall into patterns: obvious patterns, sometimes so startling she wondered who designed them.

The place she now lived in seemed to her a place without beginning. Without end. Without rise and fall. It was something else. She did not understand the ground she walked on, the air she breathed. Was this what they meant by the word *alien*? Alien: a person who does not understand the place she is in. Snow was falling on the St. Norbert streets. Snow is a story that breaks off from heaven and falls down at random, she thought. Snow longs to be whole again. It longs for its origins and cannot remember when it was together. It has fallen on an unknown country. If there is a little wind, the snowflakes dance during their descent.

She recalled walking home from school, across the mountain. She was fifteen. There was a blizzard. Thick snowflakes filled the entire air, rushing from one mountain to another. She could not see. The road was no longer visible. She did not know whether she was walking into the desert tundra, forever to perish, or home. There was fear. Wanderers had been lost in these mountains since time immemorial. Their bones had been found in the spring, lying among the sheep. Suddenly headlights appeared behind her out of the snow. A car door opened and she was pulled in. Saved. She looked to see who her rescuer was: it was Fleming, the Danish fellow. Once again, bad luck.

The church in Stadur was cold the afternoon mass was again sung in Adalvík, after twenty years of standing empty. The day everyone arrived together in a coach for a reunion. People wore skin-lined jackets in the pews because there was no heat. A small kerosene camp heater stood on the floor in front of the altar. Jakob the priest prayed from behind the small communion railing. On the walls, the oil lamps tried to compete with the summer sun that never sets in the Arctic.

The wooden walls of the church had become attuned to silence. They echoed the silence of desertion. People could tell there were ghosts: and had the curious sensation that *they themselves were the ghosts come to haunt the place where they once lived*. Reynir sat in the first pew, against the wall by the window. He had his accordion in his lap. People sang from little black hymnals with woollen sweaters draped around their shoulders. On the lectern a frayed guestbook lay open and blank. No names were written in the pages for twenty years. The stairs up to the choir loft creaked.

She sat in the second pew on the eastern side. Next to her sat a man who had become her lover when they met in Greece: the writer who had settled in Athens. Hákon the choir director looked back over his shoulder. He was a friend of the writer's other lover, the violinist who had moved to Austria. There would be talk of triangles and quadrangles. She played dumb, for lack of a better idea. Halldór the red-cheeked school teacher sat behind them. He had taught them geometry when they were children.

She liked the way the snow fell in Canada. It did not come straight down, but meandered in the air for a long time before settling. She watched one snowflake float in spirals, then up a bit, to the left, up again, down. This could go on for ten minutes before the flake joined the others on the white bundle below. At night streetscrapers in St. Norbert amused themselves by scraping the streets. They scraped down to the pavement and left mountains of packed snow cakes in front of the houses for the inhabitants to dig aside in the morning with useless tin shovels that folded under the impact of hard ice.

At the Adalvík reunion, after the mass people hung about outside the church. Wild angelica flowers reached up to their knees. A number of people were standing looking at the water in the bay. One by one the ripples gently licked the stones on the shore. Around the church, old gravestones leaned with the weather into the mountains.

The first time a rumor came that she would go to America occurred when she was eight. She told her friend Sjöfn. They had a game of exchanging all their clothes, including underwear and socks. Sjöfn pulled her into the street and pushed her in front of all passers-by crying out: *she's going to America*. Sjöfn pushed her into Jöi's grocery store and announced: *she's going to America*. The customers turned and looked at her. She was standing in her white jacket, embarrassed, playing imbecile for lack of a better idea. Many years later she got a letter from Sjöfn, posted in Ohio. She looked for a return address but found none. Evidently Sjöfn herself had gone to America.

It was said that Reynir the organist was a lucky piece of driftwood on the beach of the Vestfirdings. He was handy with several musical instruments and could, at one go, play for both the mass and the dance. The dance that night was held in the schoolhouse at Saebólsgrundir. Reynir pumped the accordion without pause all night. Like the midnight sun, he would not set.

They got their dance partners by matching halves of verses. The man who had the last two lines to go with her first two lines turned out to be Halldór the schoolteacher. Once again, bad luck. He was fond of the polka and they danced the polka for an hour. Then she sat down in the hall among the smiling black swans: the elderly women in their national costumes, seldom worn any more. She felt out of place in her white dress, purchased in Toronto.

She went outside during a lull in the dancing. A number of Adalvíkings had gathered on the grass tufts where the mountains began to rise a short distance away. It was the middle of the night, but still bright as day. A feeling of dusk pervaded the silent air. Reynir had taken his accordion out and Baldur, the priest's grandson, had brought a guitar. They were singing. Their mismatched voices sounded clearly in the stillness and echoed across the valley below.

It was a little chilly. She made her way across the tufts slowly, savoring the fresh air. Adalvík: where she liked to be alone among the singing of the ghosts. They did not see her. Many were busy covering up the left ear, the one facing the wind.

Those were the tufts of grass she ran across one day when she was twelve, very fast. She had the sudden notion that she wanted to be on the next Olympic swimming team and started training the same day. She ran the four miles from home to the sulphuric swimming pool, swam for two hours without stopping, racing from one end to the other. Then she ran the four miles back. She did not get as far as the Olympic team: she got sick instead and lay in bed all next day.

How the snow in St. Norbert was floundering, undecided whether to go back up or come down for good. The flakes blew in swirls and patterns in the gentle gusts of wind. Oblivious to the cold, they swam about in the air.

The streetscrapers came and broke the peaceful quiet of this French-Canadian town. Clamorous machines lumbered up and down the road with scathing noise. Those monsters left mountains of brown snow cakes behind them. Children in moon boots who came out of yellow schoolbuses could barely climb over the ice mountains to get home. They wiggled up on their tummies, thick arms and legs clinging to protruding ice shelves. She stood on the other side watching. In case one of these little balls missed its footing. But they all made it over, like diligent winter ants.

As she stood, the singing of the Adalvíkings swirled in her head. It was still the middle of the night and the Adalvíkings were singing under the open sky. The sun, that had been sleeping on top of Hornbjarg mountain for a while, began to rise. Suddenly the eastern sky, the sea, the stones, the hair of the singers, became drenched in gold. It was for this moment everyone had come back, she thought. *For this moment when the sun begins to ascend and the earth becomes a stone garden drenched in gold.*

The Adalvíkings were singing fatherland songs. They started up on something from Hákon's *Gravestone Suite:*

> Sun sinks in the sea
> Showers the mountain peaks with gold
> Swans fly full of song
> South towards the warm wind

Blossoms gently sway
Smile in tender oblivion
When this evening peace descends
The most beautiful of all is Adalvík

That was from the tombstone of Einar the poet.

--- ❖ ---

INSOMNIA

HE LAY IN HIS small bed unable to sleep. The tiny room was very dark, for its only window let in very little of the moonlight that was probably there. It was a clear night, he knew that. The last thing he did before retiring was go outside. He stood on his porch, hands in his pockets, and looked at the newly fallen darkness. It was early spring. The warmth in the air felt like a gentle caressing hand after the harsh winter. The snow had all melted away.

It was a moment he needed, those minutes on the porch late at night. The children were upstairs in bed by then, all four of them. His aged mother was in her room. She retired early, claiming her bones could not hold her up after evening snack. She spent her days making yarn on the spindle. No wonder her bones collapsed on her: that was altogether too stiff a posture to assume for so many hours every day. In that hard chair, too.

His wife came out and stood next to him on the porch. She said nothing, just stood there. She never said anything. Actually, he did the talking for two. She was a good woman, just a little on the quiet side. Well, what could he expect, with the cares of four children on her hands, one of whom was not so bright. That was another matter, another matter altogether.

As he lay in his bed he listened to his wife's quiet breathing. The house slept. It seemed as if the very wood in the walls slept. He slowly removed the quilt that covered him and carefully maneuvered himself out of bed. The wooden box they slept in creaked. The woman stirred momentarily, turned her head and slept on. He rose, grabbed his housecoat that lay on the chair and put it on. Tiptoeing in his slippers, he parted the curtains that separated the bedroom from the study, closed them behind him and went to the bay window.

Now he could see there was bright moonlight on the night air. Stars glistened up there like dewdrops. He had a comfortable leather-clad chair by the window and sat down in it. This was where he spent a good part of his nights. Often he read. Behind the chair he had a large bookcase with volumes in it he had yet to peruse. Gifts. Thank heaven for well-meaning friends.

Insomnia no longer bothered him. When he was young it did. That was because he was afraid of the dark then. Whatever possessed him to be afraid of the dark? Elves? Trolls? Bogeymen? Ghosts? Perhaps ghosts. It was all fantasy, and not very useful fantasy at that. No, but now he almost welcomed his own wakefulness. It was peace. A dark and solitary peace.

Of course he was tired, that was the problem with not sleeping. Yet the older he grew, the less sleep he seemed to need. One of nature's benevolent gestures. Then there was the pain. That was the worst of it, something he could do without. A pain in his bowels that kept him from relaxing. Perhaps there was something to be said for pain: it keeps you alert. But then, alert for what? It was not as if the army were around the bend, approaching.

On the windowsill in front of him he had various mementos of trips he had taken. Here was a pen given to him by a friend in Manitoba who was trying to be a novelist. A glass from another friend trying to be an editor. Ha! Somehow he was not beyond making funny remarks to himself in the still of the night, while his family slept. Actually Jón was a pretty good editor, all things considered. Even though the man refused to print the last piece of scribble he sent him.

He turned on the small lamplight by the shelves. It was good to divert the mind by visiting someone else's.

He opened the glass door to the bookcase and pulled out a thick volume recently acquired from a friend — an engineer in Chicago. *The Works of Sir Walter Scott.* Sitting down again in his leather chair, he opened the book at the place of the bookmark.

That man, this Walter Scott, was incredibly verbose. He went on and on as if he had all the time in the world. Heaven knows we do not have all the time in the world. The years go by, wrinkles gather on your face, hair turns grey, joints get stiff and bony looking. The heart beats faster, the bowels refuse to work. No, life is one long decline from the pinnacle of ignorance. Not like this new poet, the American T.S. Eliot, who never used enough words. There was an obscure fellow, not entirely readable.

The glow of the lamp was very slight, but added to the natural light emanating from the window, it was bright enough to read by. Too much light was unnecessary. It would penetrate the flimsy curtains that hung between him and his wife. She would wake up and then both of them would be tired in the morning. It was enough that only one of them did not sleep. Someone had to run the show.

In the utter quiet the sound of every page he turned seemed like thunder cutting through the night. His own breathing seemed too noisy, the whistling in his nostrils far too evident at night like this. He looked up from the book and fell into an aimless stare. Perhaps he should scribble another poem. No, not now. There were too many of them altogether. It was getting out of hand and Jón was refusing to print them anyway. This had to stop.

In the midst of this inconclusive reverie, a slight tap could be heard from the window. Was he dreaming? Another tap, this time as if from a fingernail rapping the glass. He stood up and peered out the window. Sure enough, the outline of a face was clear and a hand waving at him. Who the devil could that be? At this hour.

He carefully opened the door of the study and closed it behind him. Gently stepping across the wooden floor of the dining room, he slowly opened the front door and stepped out onto the porch. There was his friend Tómas from the village coming towards him. Was he hurt? No, just a little bent over.

Tómas grabbed him by the shoulder.

"We knew you'd be up," the guest whispered. "You're always up. We have something to share with you."

On saying this the fellow held up a bottle of Scotch, not entirely full.

"Have one, old man," Tómas whispered and handed him the flask.

He stood in his housecoat on the porch in the middle

of the night, confronting a man with a flask, and could not keep from laughing. Checking over his shoulder to see that the front door of his house was indeed closed, he took the bottle.

"You are such a persuasive fellow," he said, putting the bottle to his lips and taking a round gulp. "Have you ever thought of going into politics?"

"Join us," Tómas insisted in a harsh whisper. "There are three of us, the other two are over there in the trees. There's me, Jónas and Karl. We're going to pay a call on Edward next door and then over to Reynir's place."

He put his finger to Tómas's lips and ordered him to shut up.

"Let me see what I can do," he whispered. "Just hold it there and don't move."

With this he slowly opened the door and sneaked back into his study. There he found his baggy pants, which he put on over his pyjamas, and strung the suspenders over his shoulders. In his bare feet he stole out again, gently closing the door behind him. By the front entrance, he took his jacket off the hook, put it on and set the hat he always wore on his head. Then he fitted his cold feet into a pair of worn-out shoes and was back on the porch in minutes.

Tómas led the way down the path into the trees that bordered his land. There they found the other two men reclining against a trunk.

"So there you are you juveniles," he greeted them.

In response they gave him a laugh and a flask.

"There's a shipment of liquor that just came in," Jónas insisted. "We couldn't just sit on it, that was impossible. We waited mighty long for this order."

"Well let's get out of the vicinity before the sky falls down on us here," he said impatiently, pushing his friends on.

They filed onto the road and when well out of hearing began to sing.

They were unsuccessful at rousing Edward. Partly this was because the bedroom was not directly accessible from the outside. Short of going into the house and picking him out of bed, they were unable to get him away. After giving up there they rattled to the adjacent farm where Reynir lived. There the lights were on and since Reynir lived alone it was no problem to simply walk in on him and offer him a little sport. They planted themselves outside his window and sang "We Are Heroes" in harmony, until Reynir came out and invited them in. The rest of the night they spent sitting around Reynir's table polishing off six flasks of Scotch and all the commentary that remained in their minds.

By four-thirty he announced it was time to go. A bit of morning milking and feeding was imminent. He left his friends, who were in any case fading away rapidly, and began walking across the fields towards his own home. The narrow tinge of morning was coloring the eastern horizon. A touch of bright red, then orange, then pink, then blue. Dark blue, lighter blue, turquoise. He walked unsteadily but with determination. There was a chilly breeze — the one that always chased him home at this time of morning.

He performed the first tasks of the day before going back into the house. Filling the troughs for the cows, he spoke to them each one, bidding them good morning and mumbling under his breath. Then he went to the house, left his shoes by the front entrance where he had found them, and hung his jacket back on the hook with his hat. Entering the study, he took off his pants and placed them back on the chair. The lamp was still glowing — he had forgotten to put it out. This he did, then snuck in through the curtains to the bedroom, found his way into bed and fell sound asleep.

About an hour later his wife roused him. He was loath to awaken, just when he had fallen into a deep coma. He half opened his eyes and heard her say something indistinct. She handed him a cup of hot coffee. He raised himself on his elbow, took the cup and drank from it. He leaned back with his head against the headboard. Another day. Just another day. His head felt full of steel and his body like wash strung out on a line.

He could hear the children screaming and yelling in the kitchen. They were fighting over a bit of butter. The old woman, his mother, was coming in from the water pump with more water. One of the boys ran outside and the grandmother called after him in her high-pitched aging voice. His wife was at the study door preventing one of them from rushing in to wake him up. He closed his eyes. Stars swam in his vision.

His wife parted the curtains and came in with a small pile of linen in her arms. She bent down and put it on the chest under the window. Straightening up again she turned to look at him where he lay crookedly in bed, half sitting, half lying down, his hand on the cup of coffee at his side. He looked back at her with one eye open, one eye closed. Oh well, he must have brought in a sweltering aroma of stale Scotch.

"How did you sleep?" she asked him gently.

"Well," he hastened to answer. "I slept like a log this time."

"Good," she said, nodding her head. "Good."

She went out again. He tried to work up the stamina to get up. Doubtless there were newly baked biscuits in the kitchen. Surely she was aware of everything, surely she was. These women never say anything. They just go about their business and pretend they don't know a thing. Just as well. Then he was in no hurry to account for himself. And besides, what was there to say? What could she say?

He got up. She deserved a poem someday. He made a mental note of it. Someday, a poem just for her.

THE SONG OF THE
REINDEER

THE GLASS IN THE WINDOW behind the iron bars
appeared white, but it was just the fog of the morning.
The view was veiled in a gauze-like mist. Before the
paleness of early day, Edda's silhouette seemed like a
black shadow. She tried to look over the harbor but
could see nothing. She was tired. There had been calls
and senseless arguments out in the halls all night and
she had not slept. In the morning she was humming a
thoughtless tune to herself to stay awake. "He-ere I
si-it. He-ere I sit," she hummed.

Outside, behind that white veil that held the sleepy
town in its folds, there was another world. But it was
not the northern fjords or the rooftops of Akureyri she
thought of. It was the past. She was locked in the future
now, or so it seemed. The white walls and steel table

of the future surrounded her, crisp and solid. Sometimes in the night she could see her own reflection in
the window glass. It was broken by the iron lattice, cut
into squares. Nonetheless, the face was there. Her
short hair resembled a helmet.

Bogga came into the room with her pack of ciga-
rettes and a large black lighter. She had not combed
her hair and still wore last night's shirt. Her long brown
locks stood out in disarray and her huge black-rimmed
glasses hung precariously on the edge of her nose.

"Hi," Bogga said.

"Hi," Edda mumbled in reply. "Didn't you sleep?"

"Sleep? What stupid damned nonsense."

"They should hang those bastards," Edda concurred.

"Did you hear what they said?" Bogga added irritably.

"Yea. I heard."

Bogga sat down at the round table and lit up. Edda
stayed by the window looking out at nothing. She
wasn't at all clear how she got to be one of the only two
women in the country officially labelled as *criminals*.
There were so few criminals in the country, and so very
few of them women, that the women's jail in Akureyri
was also used as a drunk tank. The police went about
the streets at night picking up alcoholics and dumping
them into a room below stairs where they could sleep

it off on a cot. Especially on weekends the jail was noisy and unpleasant.

She tried to think. The past. The reindeer. What had happened? How did it happen again? It was all so inconclusive somehow. No. Maybe another time she would have the picture clear. She started humming again. "In the peaceful gra-ave, the silent inmates know no sorrow," she sang softly. An old folk tune.

"Oh stop it," Bogga pestered.

"Ok, ok," Edda broke in.

They were silent. It was a long weekend holiday. The kind of weekend when drinking goes on for two and three days at a time. The room below was continually being resupplied with new drunks as soon as the old ones were ready to go. They came in noisily, squawked at one another, called out, made ugly sounds and then passed out.

A hoarse and dizzy sounding man's voice suddenly roared from the hall outside the room below.

"Simon! Oh Simon! Who calls?"

Another man's voice broke in.

"Where are you Simon!"

"Here."

"Is it you Simon? Whom are you talking to?"

"I'm talking to myself!" the first voice guffawed.

"How is it with you?" said the other, in mock politeness. "How disgusting you look! What a pest to mankind you are!"

"Yes," replied the first caller pretending to sound apologetic. "I'm a pest to all living things. Why am I such a pest?!"

Edda and Bogga looked at each other in exasperation.

"Damned rotten idiots," Bogga mumbled.

They could hear heavy and unsteady footsteps in the hall. A sickly deep sing-song emanated from a third man's voice.

"Give me the fifth of February again," he muttered.

"Is it you Simon?" the first voice called out.

"Don't be ridiculous," the sickly voice whispered back.

There was a loud bump. Someone ran into the hall. Then it was quiet again.

Edda had trained herself to tune out when the noise started. There were memories, more pleasant than the present and more certain than the future. The second voice started up again.

"Last night I had the singular pleasure of conversing with a woman," the man said in exaggerated intimacy. "I am a man of the world, which is to say, a man with a good head but in disgustingly immoral shape."

"Say," the sickly voice replied. "When a girl is sixteen summers old and a boy sixteen winters old, are they the same age?"

"I am sworn to silence," said the intimate voice.

The man who had started calling on Simon broke in.

"He who sins in one thing sins in all things," he announced prophetically.

"She was married!" squealed the intimate voice.

"Simon!" the first called again.

"When I read it I got a heart attack and dropped the newspaper on the floor," continued the intimate one.

The chattering faded from Edda's hearing as she returned her gaze out through the window. The whiteness was beginning to clear up. She could see the outline of a few nearby gables. She tried to focus on the event that brought her to this unpleasant place. The reindeer hunt took place during the Christmas leave. There must have been at least thirty reindeer. They lay spread over the whole plateau and it was impossible to get a good aim. The animals had to be herded to another location first. When they raised their sticks and threw stones, the reindeer took off at a run in the direction of the eastern mountains. Óli got in their way and took a few shots at the herd. One of the reindeer fell but Óli kept running after the rest. Edda remained well enough behind not to be caught in the path of the bullets. When Óli ran on, she followed along the trail. There was blood on the tracks.

"Those horrible savages!" someone screamed.

It was Bogga. Edda turned around and saw her cellmate leaning on her elbows, covering her ears with clenched fists.

"Don't let it get to you," Edda advised.

"How the hell is a person supposed to get any peace in this place!" Bogga yelled desperately.

A sudden silence fell on the men in the hall and the lower room. The two women waited, but there was no sound.

"They heard you," Edda whispered.

Bogga lit another cigarette. Edda turned back to the window. She could now see the nearest streets as the fog lifted slowly. Something moved in one of them. Perhaps a truck.

Óli had left his rifle on the ground beside the wounded reindeer. She stopped there and saw the spastic breathing in the grass hillocks. The herd was scattering before Óli's onslaught and one bull was lagging behind. It was clearly broken in the leg. It looked like the break had occurred just above the shank. The leg seemed to dangle and sway up to the animal's back and down under its stomach. Óli approached it and the bull jutted its horns at him. Edda yelled.

"Óli! Get away! You don't have your gun!"

The reindeer attacked. Óli took the horns in both his hands and the two of them pulled and pushed back and forth with all their beastly strength. Edda grabbed the rifle where it lay in the grass. The animal beside her breathed more calmly. A wave of drowsiness had overcome it.

"Hey!"

Someone whispered almost inaudibly behind her. Edda turned to look. Bogga was gone and someone stood behind the white bars that separated her room from the hall. It was a young man. He was wearing sunglasses, a dark overcoat and a striped tie over a blue shirt. His dark blond hair was blown about as if he had just come in from a storm.

"Hey!" he whispered again.

She recognized him.

"Hilmar!" she whispered back incredulously.

"Shh!" he hissed.

"How'd you get in here?" Edda asked in surprise. "For Christ's sake!"

"Edda, hey, how're you doing?" Hilmar said in a low friendly voice.

She looked out through the bars suspiciously. No one was there. She crossed the room carefully to the visitor.

"What on earth are you doing here?" she whispered again.

"Listen, I came north. I had to get real drunk to be put in the tank for a night. I smashed a window in the salesbooth on Odd's Street. I wanted to see you."

"Quiet!" Edda interrupted under her breath when she heard a noise in the hall.

They listened for the footsteps. After a while it was quiet again.

Hilmar was observing Edda on the other side of the bars.

"So I've come to the women's jail in Akureyri," he said in mild disbelief and looked around him. "Is that white jersey yours?"

"What do you think, of course it's mine," Edda replied frustrated. "They're not stupid enough to give us convicts' clothes."

"How many of you are there?" he asked.

"Two. My term is up next August."

"Is it difficult, hey?" Hilmar asked her sympathetically.

"Of course it's difficult," she blurted back. Unlike her, she felt like crying in her frustration. "I can't think any more. I'm completely blank. The drunks are dumped in here on weekends and we don't get any sleep."

They stood on each side of the white bars silently for a while. Hilmar put the tips of his fingers against the side of her head in a caressing gesture.

"Heida's fine," he said to change the subject. "She misses you."

"Tell her the same, will you?" Edda answered gratefully. "Is she growing fast?"

"Like a geyser. Lots of attention."

"I get to go south next weekend," Edda assured him. "They're taking us on the morning plane and we go back on the last flight that night."

"They say this is a white-collar jail," Hilmar suddenly said looking around again. "For money swindlers and such. Doesn't look so bad to me. Pretty decent, if you ask me. You even have a rug on the floor here. They feed you well, don't they? Sure they do."

"The women who work here are nice," Edda concurred. "That's about all. Hey," she added as if in afterthought after a brief silence, "you can't stay here forever. I'll just get into trouble. Get lost, will you."

"Sure," Hilmar said quickly under his breath. "Don't be sore. I just wanted to see you."

He had almost stopped whispering and put his hand on Edda's cheek. Through the opening between bars, he kissed her gently. They heard someone in the hallway again and stiffened up.

"Beat it Hilmar!" Edda whispered.

He quickly walked out of sight, so carefully his footsteps could not be heard.

In the ensuing silence Edda went back to the window. The air had cleared considerably. She could see the streets clearly and the doorways of the houses. The roofs jutted deep green, rusty brown and red into the white sky. Curtains were folded neatly and in one gable window a light glowed feebly. A black and white bird that looked like a gull soared low over the harbor water and knifed up again over the town. It had long narrow wings and its bill looked like a scissor that opened and shut as it approached the water again. Someone protested confusedly somewhere else in the building. The voice was dazed with old drunkenness.

"What the hell, I'm not staying in any EDDU-jail!" the man declared.

She had heard it before. They were naming the women's jail after her because no one had received such a long term before.

She heard Bogga return, dragging her feet.

"He's gone?" Bogga asked, looking around.

"Yea," Edda said without looking back.

"He sure takes chances, that guy," Bogga muttered.

"That's his way," Edda said. "You don't get anything for sitting around obedient and stupid," she added irritably.

"Soon we can go to sleep," Bogga claimed. "The rest of them are leaving."

"Bloody bastards," Edda mumbled to herself.

"Did you hear what they said?" Bogga asked testingly.

"Fools," Edda snapped back. "Yes I damn well did."

They were quiet again. The moments crawled forward. The gull took another dash at the water.

Óli was holding the reindeer bull off with his left hand while he reached for the knife in his belt. Edda had the rifle in her hands. She was carrying extra bullets for him and stuck one into the compartment, locked it and pushed it in. She left the wounded animal behind and threaded the hillocks with careful speed in the direction of the attacking bull. Óli took the knife out of the holster and with a swift movement plunged it into the animal's spine. The bull collapsed before him immediately, the legs buckling under the sudden loss of control. Just at that moment, Edda pulled the trigger of the rifle she had aimed at the two of them. The bullet flew off with a ringing knock. She could feel the pressure against her collarbone where she had rested the rifle head.

One of the drunks below started singing suddenly.

"My si-ilent accomplice, do we not repea-eat ourselves? Have we not every-thing twi-ice, my silent vice?" he intoned.

"What they don't think up!" Bogga exclaimed in condemnation.

The first drunkard spoke up again as if from a deep sleep.

"Simon!" he called, "is it you?"

"Who calls?" yelled the second voice.

"Life has given me what I love the most," said the man who repeatedly asked for Simon. "Myself."

"Ha ha!" a new voice laughed loudly.

The singer started up on a tune again.

"The memory of lo-ove, is happiness twi-ice, my silent accomplice. Tell me one thing but think another-er," he sang.

The voice trailed off into a falsetto and a laugh.

When Óli heard the shot, he looked over his shoulder stunned. She lowered the rifle and saw how the bullet had gone into the reindeer's forehead. The animal's nostrils and horns were spotted with large slabs of blood. Óli stood as still as a stone looking at her without expression. His feet were spread wide apart and he held the knife in his clenched fist without moving. The furrow between his eyebrows, that looked like an eagle's claw prints, seemed more pronounced than ever. His long curls stood out in all directions like the horns of a reindeer bull. His lips were pressed strangely and the blue eyes gazed out like question marks. His white pullover was stained with red and brown and his jeans were muddy. Then he too collapsed where he stood.

All she could think of was how rare it is for a hunter to get two in one shot. They said only Island-Magnús and Ísólfsskála-Gudmundur were so lucky, and sometimes Marardals-Helgi. How absurd that it should happen to her.

A man came walking under the window. His dark coat flew in the wind but he did not bother to button it. He had his right hand in his pocket and moved quickly toward the harbor. He was wearing sunglasses even though it was just about to rain. It looked as if he was heading for a trawler moored near the warehouse, *Reykjanes KE* it was called. The man looked over his shoulder up at the window. It was Hilmar. They had let him out. He ran his fingers through his hair as if to steady it in the wind.

She heard the men in the hall again. Drunks were so absurdly formal when they railed like that, and melodramatic. One of them was muttering in a deep voice.

"Oh the endless unhappy masses!" he railed. "One word and hope vanishes."

"Yes we are all uninvited guests," concurred another voice.

"No!" said the first. "We are romantic soldiers."

The voice that had complained about a married woman and reading the paper started up again.

"The thing is, dear friends, one should never look

back. Don't look back. All you'll see is your execu-
tioner," he advised.

"Why don't you stop this nonsense?" a guard's voice
suddenly said.

"Because," said the one who had just spoken, "it
happened to Lot's wife, did it not? She looked back and
see what happened to her!"

Bogga was chain-smoking at the round table when
Edda turned to look. Her white perforated clogs
clanged rhythmically against the steel foot of the table.
Soon there would be peace in the building. The men
were leaving one by one. Someone passed below in a
crumpled suit, walking as if he had just seen a ghost.
They all looked like that the morning after. Their legs
were stiff and they kept their heads facing straight
forward as if the neck were made of steel and they could
look neither left nor right.

Now Edda could see over the town clearly. The gull
was nowhere in sight. Perhaps it had found a herring
on the pier and flown away with it. Hilmar had turned
a corner and disappeared. She started softly on her
song again. "In the peaceful gra-ave, the silent inmates
know no sor-row, and if they find no rest, they wander
on the earth tomor-row," she hummed.

"Stop it for Pete's sake," Bogga pleaded.

Edda did not turn around. She did not stop either.

No one tells the reindeer they can't sing, she thought. And they do. They do sing. She had heard them.

"Life is for me a bitter drink," said an unhappy voice in the hall. "And still I have to take it in drop by drop, minute by minute! You know who said that? No, you probably don't. Time, stand still so I will. Oh I want to stand absolutely still, just for a moment . . ."

The mumbling became incomprehensible. They heard a door slam in the far end of the hall. There was a scream. Edda peered out the window.

"What was that scream?" Bogga asked surprised.

"Nothing," Edda said. "It was just a gull. The window is open, you know."

"Oh," Bogga answered with sarcastic emphasis.

Then it was quiet.

THE GOOSE GIRL

SHE COMES DOWN the mountainside above Castlegar, B.C., in her flat shoes. She walks slowly because of the geese. Three large geese, two white and one grey, follow her. The geese wobble awkwardly on their webbed feet, raising dust on the path beside the road as they drag themselves forward. It is the middle of March. The snow has melted but the rains have not begun. The land is dry and still denuded: grass is not yet green and leaves have not sprung. In her hand she holds a birchwood walking stick. With it she keeps the geese from straying into the road where cars frequently drive by.

Around the girl and her three geese the mountains rise in layers. Higher up on the slopes there is snow and skiing is still possible. Below her lies the town with its dusty wooden houses and small motels and gas stations. Motorists on their way between Calgary and Vancouver drive through these valleys, past the pulpmills spewing odorous clouds into the air and log jams on the rivers. She walks this way twice a day; once in the early morning and once at evening. On both occasions she can see the deeply gilded edges the rising and falling sun brings to the world.

She lives in a shack on the higher northern mountainside with her ailing father and their small flock of geese. It is a shack her father built when he was young and settled with his wife in the interior of British Columbia to work in forestry. It consists of one large room. Along the western wall is a kitchen counter. Two sofas fill the corner of the north wall and a reading chair stands in the northeastern corner. In the middle of the room a wood-burning stove nurses its glowing ashes all day. The southern wall is taken up by a staircase leading to a balcony that overlooks the whole room. On this balcony she has a cot to sleep on and a crocheted blanket her mother once made. Her father lies permanently ill on the north sofa below.

Her parents came from Denmark to British Columbia thirty-five years ago and reclusively settled where no one else lived. She was born in this shack. Castlegar and its regions is the only world she knows. As far back as she remembers, she has fetched water, chopped wood, grown vegetables in the garden, made materials, crocheted blankets, sewn together strips of leather and tended the geese they have always had. She went to school in town and finished high school, but her mother died and she took on the work left undone in her absence. Now her father is unable to do his share as well, and she does the work of two.

Beside the town of Castlegar lies another village of several very small houses with well-tended gardens around. This is the Doukhobor settlement and the destination of her twice daily treks down the mountainside. She comes to buy from them vegetables and eggs. They give her fabric and yarn and she makes material for them in return on a loom her father once built. She crosses a narrow creek from the main avenue and finds herself walking along winding, thin roads between houses. To her left, down a wider street and across another small bridge, a huge cedar building towers into the overcast air. This is the Doukhobor Community Center. She looks to her left when she crosses the street. To her it is an impressive building and she hopes it will not be burned down by factions in the Doukhobor community.

It is early evening and she walks listlessly, trailing her birchwood stick in the dust. She can feel the dampness in the air through her thin grey short-sleeved sweater. A small wind catches her blue skirt.

Her collar-length light brown hair flows gently along her cheeks. Across the ravine she can see the buildings of Selkirk College. It is a place she wanted to go. To learn something, be someone in the world. But she cannot because her father's illness is long and slow. He has nowhere to go if she does not care for him. She can see young people run across the College grounds and drive away in cars.

Peter the Great is waiting at his front door. His name is Peter, but she has added the nickname. A short man with a large stomach and round face, he is prominent in the Doukhobor community. It is Peter who makes her exchanges with Doukhobor households possible and she has known him all her life. As she comes up to the house, he opens his arms wide.

"Dear little Danish girl with the geese!" he calls to her affectionately. "And how is your father today?"

"Thank you," she tells him, "not better, unfortunately."

"Your poor father," he consoles her, shaking his head and folding his hands. They go to the back where a sack of potatoes has been made up for her to take home.

"Can you carry this yourself all the way back?" he asks concernedly. She nods.

"Now," Peter informs her, "I have a request!" She looks up inquiringly. He gives her a pointed look.

"We are having a conference!" he almost shouts.

"A what?" she asks uncertainly.

"A conference!" he shouts. It seems to be a very jovial matter to him. "A conference," he goes on, "with four writers from the Soviet Union coming here to our Community Center! There will be many people coming here, my friend, and we need you for something!"

"I can't imagine what you need me for," she answers almost dismissively.

"Well, I will tell you," Peter lectures in reply. "We will have an evening of music, food, dance, readings, presentations. We want you to make a presentation!"

"What do you mean?" she asks worriedly.

"I mean, we want you to make a speech!"

"A speech?"

"Yes! A speech!" he yells happily, grasping her shoulders with both hands.

"You know I can't do that," she refuses. She is not as delighted as he is.

"Of course you can!" he shouts. "Only a minute long, my friend, only a minute, or thirty seconds," he adds reassuringly.

"What's the use of a thirty-second speech?" she laughs.

"The use is," he answers in seriousness, "that we have greetings to the Soviet visitors from the Doukhobor community. I give them myself! But they are not in Russia, they are in Canada. And in Canada there are many more people than those of us who are of Russian descent. In this area there are people of all kinds, as you know."

"And?" she prompts him on.

"And! We want you to give the greetings from those who live here who are not of Russian descent." He leans his head back and observes her as if from a high distance, pleased with his work.

In the end she agrees to deliver the greeting. She has never stood in front of people before and is not in the least certain of her ability to carry it through. But if she is part of the proceedings, she will be part of the conference. She has never attended a conference before. She has never seen writers from the Soviet Union before. It will be a dream to be in the Community Center while all this is going on and she part of it, she thinks, and walks back to her father's shack with a new buoyancy.

The evening settles with a flat greyness she is used to. Approaching the shack, the ground feels wet under her feet. Some planks she placed on the mud have slipped off track. The shack stands at the bottom of a small incline. She walks in and places the potatoes on the kitchen table. The three geese that have taken the walk with her scamper about the yard. She throws them some crumbs. Her father lies still in the falling light. He looks over at her arrival silently, his blue eyes surprisingly large. He has not lost the good colour in his cheeks, from years of mountain walking.

She fetches a glass of water and brings it to his bedside. By the bed she has placed a small stool, covered with her mother's old embroidery. She sits and gently places the glass to her father's lips. He sips slowly, carefully, breathing only half perceptibly. She can see his heart has become weak from lying still for many weeks. He half closes his eyes and his eyeballs roll up until only the whites of his eyes are showing. It is his estranged form of sleep. She sits still, waiting. The geese can be heard screeching in the distant corner of the yard.

Her thirty-second speech is rehearsed over many times as dusk falls in and the quiet of the little shack engulfs them both. It is a most awkward assignment. She is conscious of her own shyness and lack of experience. To make matters worse, all she has to wear is what she wears every day. She will not cut a splendid figure but she will be there. The call of the world on the young woman with the glass of water and the geese at the door, sitting still at her father's bedside, is after all, an irresistible call.

The Doukhobor Community Center is simply an empty shell of great size. Inside it has only one room of extreme proportions and high ceiling and a basement with a kitchen. All is empty. When people fill the center, benches are brought out. The benches are stiff and uncomfortable, made of polished slabs of wood. On the day of the conference, she comes into the Center in her flat shoes and seats herself at the very back of the room on a separate bench against the back wall. In the front of the room benches are lined up and filled with people from the College and the Doukhobor community. Facing the audience, at a separate table, are six speakers, each with their own microphone. Those must be the writers, she thinks.

She listens to each speaker who stands up and delivers a brief talk. There are two women and four men. The Soviet writers only speak Russian and since the people from the College do not understand them, they have brought a translator. She observes the young Russian who has come from the Soviet Union with the writers in order to translate what they say. She reads on the brochure that he is a member of the Soviet Academy of Sciences. He stands to the side by a microphone and translates everything said into both languages. She has never seen such easy brilliance. The way he carries his education as if it were a simple bit of crumbs for the geese. He is tall and slender, short dark hair haphazardly combed, and his movements are quick and comfortable.

That is the way she would like to be able to carry herself in front of so many people, she thinks. The day wears on. She takes her trek back to the shack and sits with her father absentmindedly. Half of what has passed at the Center has gone by her: she was too far away to hear everything. But she has seen enough to make her ill at ease. All those people have somewhere to go. She knows she does not. There is her father taking his final moments in an ill-constructed house. There are geese to keep and a vegetable garden to begin preparing. It seems as if the world is revolving without her and she will never step into the arena of human affairs.

She has promised Peter to help the Doukhobor women serve dinner at the banquet in the Center that evening. By five-thirty she is on her way again down the slopes. She tries to avoid getting her blue skirt dusty and her grey blouse shows just a small smudge from the tea she spilled. It is the best she can do, she thinks. It takes a while to convince her three geese that they cannot waddle along beside her this time. She pens them into the yard and walks away gently.

In the Center basement all tables are set up and all women have scarves on their heads. She borrows a scarf, ties it around her hair and helps set bowls and plates on the white tablecloths. Soon the guests trickle in and seat themselves. There are the customary prayers, songs and speeches, during which she hides in a corner in the kitchen. Then the women come out with immense bowls of bright orange borscht and place them at regular intervals on all the tables. She brings in bread and perogies and pours cups full of coffee, melting into the surroundings almost unnoticeably.

After dinner there are more speeches and presentations. Then all file up to the main hall for the events on the stage. Peter takes her by the arm and leads her upstairs, up to the front row where he tells her to sit down. She has never been in the front row before and finds it to be an uncomfortably visible place. But she would never contradict Peter, who has made almost everything possible for her after her father's illness came on. The Doukhobor choir sings, speeches are held at the podium up front, the Soviet writers read their poems, someone dances. Eventually she notices Peter in the wings, motioning to her that she should come backstage and prepare to give her greeting.

When she comes on the stage in front of the curtain, she finds she cannot see anything in the audience, for the light shines directly in her face. There is only pitch blackness before her: a void that is filled with a collective human soul waiting to listen to her words. She feels unspeakably awkward. Her carefully smoothed clothes feel like tatters and rags. Her hair seems to her to be littered with leaves and goose feathers and debris from the grounds around the shack. Her voice sounds harsh and exaggerated in the microphone and she feels like the geese at her door that can do nothing but screech unintelligibly and waddle back and forth on flat feet. She realizes with terror that she has forgotten her little presentation in her intimidation over the sophisticated visitor who fluidly composes translations and delivers them without a single error, and with no effort.

"I wish to extend," she begins into the microphone, "very friendly greetings to the visitors from . . . from Russia from us who live in Castlegar's surrounding regions." She has a strong sensation that what she is saying is not grammatically correct. "Those who have come here for other reasons, not the reasons that the Doukhobor people came here, also share in the gifts given by the community." To her mortification she is speaking with an accent. "And we also are very pleased of the opportunity to meet writers and trans . . . translators from the Soviet Union," she concludes. "Thank you."

As swiftly as she can she is off the stage and tiptoeing back to her seat in the front row. The next presentation is already underway when she composes herself in her seat, folds her hands in her lap and tries to calm the exaggerated heart pounding in her chest. Suddenly she realizes that the Russian translator is hurriedly running from the other side of the room, bending low so as not to interfere with the audience's view of the stage. He rushes up, kneels in front of her and grasps her hands tightly between his.

"When I saw you there," he half whispers, half shouts to her, "when I heard you . . . " He hesitates and stares intently into her eyes. "I knew . . . " Without being able to finish his sentence, he hurries back to his own seat on the other end of the row.

As soon as there is a perceptible break in the proceedings, she steals away. She has been gone too long, her father is in need of attention and she hurries out of the Center without speaking to anyone. Her heart is beating loudly all the way home. She breathes hurriedly and hard. The small stones on the road rustle under her feet and the stars glimmer all over the night sky. She does not know what to think and she does not think. When she comes into the shack, she sees her father's arm has fallen over the edge of the sofa and is hanging in midair. He is asleep and there is a rattling sound in his throat. She straightens him out, checks the fire in the stove and goes up into her cot under the crocheted blanket. There she lies awake, the world spinning in her head.

Next morning she has miraculously forgotten the events of the night before. The concerns of the day are enough to fill her mind. She kindles the stove up, puts water on the boil, helps her father wash and eat, feeds the geese and shakes out the blankets in the fresh morning air. A brilliant sun is blazing from the horizon and the pine trees are etched in deep orange. She is gratified by the beauty of her surroundings. As she places more sticks in the fire, Nader, the young boy from the Mikhail family in the Doukhobor village comes running up to the door.

"Hi," the boy shouts and walks in uninvited.

"Hello there," she answers him, pleased to see people. "What brings you here so early?"

"It's the man from Russia," the boy tells her, still panting from the run. "He asked me to tell you if you would come this morning to say goodbye."

"Come to the Center?" she asks, to be quite sure.

"Yes, I guess. You got anything to eat?" She laughs and hands him a slice of bread, which he devours.

"I'll come down to say goodbye," she assures him. "You can tell your man that from me." He runs off again and she stands in the doorway.

When her morning chores are done, she puts on her sweater and skirt, takes her walking stick from the wall where she hangs it, and opens up for the geese. They can come with her this time. She will not try to change her daily ways just because she has given a thirty-second speech in front of a real audience, she assures herself. She knows it is not possible to hope for what cannot be achieved. Be comfortable with your daily lot, her father has said to her many times. She heads down the road with her three geese in tow, quacking and getting in each other's way, making the business of moving forward awkward and slow.

At long last she comes down to the plain, crosses the creek and turns left toward the imposing building where people are milling about in the parking lot. She has obviously missed the proceedings that broke up the conference, for people are leaving in their cars. Slowly she makes her way to the door, and sneaks in, leaving her geese aimlessly wandering about the lot outside. As she comes into the auditorium, the young man from Russia who sent for her eyes her from the other side of the room. He quickly dispenses remarks to various people, dashing about his business as fast as he can.

As she stands in the middle of the room feeling lost, not knowing what she should do next, the translator has found his way to her.

"I wanted very much to see you before we go," he assures her. She smiles questioningly, and nods politely. He hands her a piece of paper.

"My address in Moscow," he tells her. He grasps her hands and holds them tightly against his chest. He is standing close to her, looking down at her puzzled face intently.

"Would you like me to write you?" she asks hesitantly, not knowing what to do about the address he has given her.

"Yes!" he whispers, "that is what I want. That is what this is for!" He smiles as if he has just looked into a room full of wonders. Someone beckons for him to come.

"Let us stay together!" he whispers, tightens his grip around her hands, and just as suddenly lets go to join his group. Before she can pull herself together, he has disappeared.

Day passes into evening and evening into night. Morning comes with its golden wings and silver voices, and she goes about her daily ways in the mountains of British Columbia. Nothing has changed for the goose girl, yet somehow everything has changed. She cannot name it, cannot see it, but something has changed. There will be no difference in her life. She will never set eyes on the man from Moscow again. She knows that and yet she can still feel the clasp of his hands. For some reason, when he left it was as if one star out of the night sky remained hanging and would not go out with all the others.

She pours the boiling water into her father's cup. Into it she places a teabag and next to it on the plate, a slice of bread. Sitting beside the ailing man, she feeds him breakfast and sings to him. He likes to hear her sing the songs of his childhood. She has been humming the tunes of her mother for many years like this, the tunes her mother taught her. The spirit her mother left behind. Somewhere among the mountains or in the night sky, the songs that made life possible for them both lay waiting.

Og går du ud at finde
hvorover stjernen står,
måske du først må vandre
i mange lange år . . .

"And if you walk out to find," she hums, "what the star is shining on; perhaps you must first wander for many long years . . . "

Her father listens with eyes closed, a slight smile on his weakened face, thinking the sky was empty and not a single spark remained.

CHEZ JEANETTE

JEANETTE WAS WONDERFUL. A tall and slender American woman with straight shoulder-length hair and a sense of humor. When she laughed her body writhed like a snake. She brought the wine and offered the taste to Ruby's mother. Ruby was very glad she did not instinctively give the glass to her brother, the only male at the table, the youngest of the three of them dining there on December twenty-sixth. That would be Boxing Day. It must have been some kind of Cabernet Sauvignon, in any case something French, but her mother declared it fit to drink and they plunged in. Between the three of them they cleaned off two bottles of wine, which was a lot. Ruby's brother was the only one who drank alcohol on a regular basis, and that would usually be Henry Weinhard beer.

That dinner must have taken a good four hours to get through. Much of that time was spent waiting for the food. They were very slow in bringing it, which meant you had more wine. But once inside *Chez Jea-nette* you didn't want to leave anyway. Perhaps Jeanette had won a lottery or inherited vast sums, but she bought a little house on the old Highway 101 on the Oregon coast at Gleneden Beach, renovated it into a quaint French country house covered in flowers and turned it into a restaurant that served dinners only after five-thirty. When you entered you saw first thing a gigantic fireplace with a splendid fire going. The wallpaper was black with small pale yellow blooms in antiquated symbolic patterns throughout.

There were white tablecloths on the tables and white cloth serviettes done in rabbit-ear fashion standing up from the wine glasses. There was even the house cat, Felix, a black female cat that went around sniffing at things.

For some reason which Ruby had not decided, it took guts to come here for the holidays. Perhaps it took guts to travel because she had the flu two weeks before departure and it only abated on Christmas day. Or, what was more likely, she had the flu because she was going to visit her family. As soon as the flu ended, a cold came on that filled her head with steel wool and kept her sneezing like a lumberjack. But, miraculously,

there were two days when she was free of both ail-
ments, or rather between them, and felt fine. Those
days were the twenty-sixth and -seventh. They took
the opportunity and went to *Chez Jeanette*, covered in
sweet pea blossoms clinging to the vines that went up
the white stucco walls of the low-lying country house
with its Cape Cod roof.

She didn't so much mind *flying* as she minded waiting in airports. Holidays were the worst times to travel
because they were the worst times to get stuck in
airports, bus terminals, train stations. The Vancouver
airport was the worst. Her brother, whom they called
Ascott because he had once wanted to change his name
to something more *aristocratic* in the English sense, had
dubbed the airport in Vancouver *Chernenco Airport*
because it was so unattractive, so *Soviet* somehow. And
coming to the Oregon coast over Christmas meant a
five-hour wait in Chernenco Airport for Ruby. There
were so many people that it was out of the question to
wait in line for a simple cup of coffee. She bought an
orange juice at a juice stand, went outside where the
limousines were coming and going with tinted windows and uniformed chauffeurs, and sat down on a
bench. It was overcast, as usual, but mild. The grass
was green. The air smelled damp and fungusy.

Ruby knew she did not entirely know herself, although she knew a few things. Among them was that

she had a problem with doing things she didn't want to do. She did things for other people. As a result sometimes she overreached and ended up either exhausted or psychologically complicated, full of resentments and irritations. Even when she agreed to visit the coast, she realized it was an *overreach*, beyond her limits, and something she should not do. But her mother's voice on the phone, plaintive, scared, unhappy, made it impossible to say no. Outright. Instead she hedged, was tentative, mentioned various difficulties, assured her she'd call her back. In the end she knew she had to go.

But that was not all. She had also agreed to meet a friend of hers in Seattle in February, only two months later. That meant another flight over the mountains of British Columbia and down the coastal range. She did not know how she had been talked into the second trip so easily. In retrospect, she realized she had even proposed it herself. To please her friend. To *please*. And why was she spending all her money, her time, her nerves and good health, just to make sure people continued to like her. More than that: so people would continue to *love* her. She could not stand being hated. To be *hated* was a fate worse than Hell. It had happened once or twice that someone actually hated her, and she suffered what seemed endlessly from the knowledge that she was *misapprehended* by someone. Seriously misjudged.

She watched the porter standing with his suitcase cart waiting for customers. She never made use of their services, not after the last time when she came through this same airport with more luggage than she could handle and too little money. The porter helped her with all her bags to the United States counter, up the escalator and across the building. In the end she realized she had only a few coins to give him for a tip. She handed them to him apologetically. The short man in his uniform looked at the pitiful collection of dimes and nickels and threw them back at her violently yelling "I didn't haul all that luggage for this!" and walked away in furious disgust. She stood there in humiliation, watching him stomp away.

For someone who hated travelling, she travelled enormously often. Airport disasters were her specialty. Once at La Guardia in New York, she was transporting part of her personal library overseas to her flat in Paris. While going through luggage inspection before boarding, her suitcase broke and all her books came tumbling out. For twenty minutes she kneeled on the airport floor picking up paperback volumes of Voltaire, Tolstoy, Marquez, Lermontov, Vonnegut, Kundera, and it occurred to her maybe it would help if she started reading some women writers. True to the resolution, when in Paris she read Colette, Sagan, Spark, Brookner, Atwood, whatever women authors she could find.

But reading women writers didn't help. She was still the same person, constantly giving herself away and keeping less and less for herself. Or was it that she derived less and less *pleasure* from *giving* as she grew older. Or, paradoxically, was it that *generosity* was becoming more and more of a *dirty word* as the Randyan age they lived in sped forward?

When Ruby's plane landed in Portland, Trinidad was there. *Trinidad* was the name they had given her mother, perhaps because they found her a little *exotic* or *sunny* or even *dark*. In any case, her mother was different and seemed to have come from a world no one else was quite familiar with. They headed straight for Trinidad's jeep. Ruby had learned to travel without luggage. She took only her toothbrush and an American Express card in case she needed to purchase anything along the way. She did not even bother to go through the tedium of acquiring U.S. currency at the bank. At one time she always took several dresses and hats and shoes with her everywhere, in case something *interesting* turned up. But nothing sociable ever came up on the Oregon coast. Just water, sand, fish and lumber. And she never met any *men* there either.

The cottage at Gleneden Beach was cold and damp from the rains. Trinidad went out back to turn on the water and Ruby cranked up the heaters in all the rooms. They stuffed newspapers and pieces of wood into the fireplace that stood in the middle of the floor and lit an afternoon fire. Alders and pines crowded the cottage, almost blocking the sun. It was often sunny on the coast, it seemed. The winds from the west blew the clouds in over the mountains and left the coastline clear. They quickly drove to Depoe Bay south of the beach and picked up a cache of fresh smoked Albacore tuna, Oregon shrimp and pickled herring. With this and a loaf of sourdough bread from the Lincoln Beach bakery they were set to spend the holidays in relative comfort.

While they waited for Ascott to arrive that evening, Ruby went to the beach. It was a tradition to walk several miles every day along the water. They used to consult a tide chart to see when the water would be low and the sand damp and firm to walk on. Low tide was also a good time for scavenging: Oregon jaspers, agates and shells of all descriptions appeared glistening among the gravel of the ocean bottom once the receding water had exposed them. Ruby no longer waited for those times. She walked whenever she felt like it. High tide was also dramatic, when the water threatened to rise to the inside edge of the beach and carve a few more inches from under the exposed cottages hanging precariously at the brink of the cliff above.

The beach cottage was a family retreat. Ruby always thought she could come here to *think things over*, that the ocean and its ageless activity somehow *induced wisdom*. But she always found the opposite to be true. Walking by the ocean simply humiliated the intellect and emptied your mind. What seemed important before became trivial in light of seagulls smashing little clam shells to smithereens and baby pelicans lying abandoned in the sand dunes unable to fly, or blobs of jellyfish left on dry land by receding waters, helpless in amoebal immobility. She never did figure out what to do about incompatible choices and paradoxes that came up in urban life. Should she engage in the politics of the journal where she worked? Should she finally *put her foot down* with her common-law husband and take the consequences? The coastline, ocean foam hurtling short distances in the wind across the white sand, seemed to laugh at such petty concerns.

The sun was low and about to set over the western horizon. The beach was peculiarly empty. People must have gone home to families for Christmas instead of coming here. Even the seabirds, those perennial creatures that squawked and quarrelled and flew gracefully over the waters to nab little fish close to the surface, were not there. Ruby speculated whether there was a change in patterns of migration for herring, cod, whales, that would prompt the disappearance of seabirds. Or perhaps there was a change in nutritional composition of the coastal waters. Perhaps pollution.

She had never seen the sands so barren of life before. She did not walk far. Instead she wandered slowly towards the north, stopped often to look at the water, and turned back early.

Ruby knew they would avoid the issue. She herself, walking on the beach in the early evening, was avoiding the issue. Ascott would arrive later and together the three of them would avoid the issue. The fact is, she said to herself on the empty, cool, December coast, *this is the first Christmas without father.* They were spending it at the beach cottage, on Ruby's insistence, so they would not have to have Christmas in the family home in the valley and sit there gawking over the gaping hole of his absence. Every time they walked through a doorway in that house, they would think *he is not here.* The Christmas dinner would be put out and *his seat would be empty.* They would try to sing a carol and his out of tune, half apologetic non singing voice *would not be in the song.* They would look at one another, the three of them, and their eyes would be blank. Their faces would be fixed in an effort not to weep like lost children. Ruby insisted she would only come down on the condition that they *not observe Christmas* and instead have a holiday at the beach, with fires in the fireplace, walks on the sand, and good books to read when it rained.

It was not so much *denial* as it was a sense that *weeping time was over*. It was time to get on with things. Ruby had felt she was moving forward and did not want to return to a place she had been in before. It would not be good for any of them. She wandered back to the cottage slowly, making her way through a path in the woods crowned with pines that lean over in the wind. The darkness of the forest under the crowns of the trees had deprived the trunks of sunlight so branches further below withered and died. When she opened the red door of the cottage she saw that Ascott had arrived. He stood in the middle of the room, in front of the fire, a red sweater in one hand and *The Wall Street Journal* in the other. On his face was his perennial smile. "Ruby!" he greeted her.

Ruby was another family nickname. It had been given to her because her lips were supposedly so *kissable* but, as usual, the connection was not clear. As she got older she saw more and more reason to *object* to it, but the name was second nature now and had stuck fast, like all the others. While Ascott drank his Henry Weinhard, Trinidad puttered about the cottage homifying it and Ruby made corrections to a review she wrote on the way to the coast while waiting at the airport and on the planes. It was pitch black at the beach. Whatever streetlights there were had been placed far from one another. Stars were always highly visible. A mile or so north of the cottage was the village of Gleneden, a collection of dilapidated cottages that no one could afford to keep in shape. Front steps were slanted from constant leaning, roofs were worn thin from frequent rains, paint was peeling off from constant ocean winds battering.

The ritual of evening news and late night tea was quickly established among the three of them. Ruby and Ascott cracked jokes and laughed at them. Ruby told funny stories of encounters with weird people at the journal. Ascott told stories of injustice at his university department. Trinidad sounded the background response, always correct, always sympathetic. It was not bad. Ruby had feared it would be strained and tense, but it was pleasant. She was mildly surprised although she could not account for her fears that the visit would be hard to take. As day succeeded day, she began to realize that it was not going to be unpleasant. They were going to slide through the holidays smoothly after all. No one would sit down to cry this time. They were not going to indulge in the sentiments of their sorrow. She felt mildly relieved.

Trinidad broke the pact in small ways, as was expected. When she saw everyone doing Christmas things, she wanted to as well. She talked of having a tree until Ruby and Ascott showed they were not interested. She could not refrain from baking and they could not keep her away from the oven, so holiday cakes appeared. Ruby had announced that she would make the dinner on Christmas Eve, and it was to be something new they had never had before. To that effect they purchased pork tenderloin which was to be stuffed with prunes and apples. But Trinidad made red cabbage on the sly and brought it out anyway, the red cabbage they always had for Christmas Eve. Ascott made an unusual Greek salad and Trinidad stood over him uncertainly critical, for no one ever ate Greek salad on that evening in her personal memory. And on the twenty-fourth, in spite of all protests to the contrary, suddenly parcels wrapped in colourful Christmas paper began to pile up on the table. Everyone had made an exception to the rule when it came to presents. Ruby looked at the pile in vague disappointment.

During the day Ascott and Ruby hiked along the beach. It was possible to walk all the way to Lincoln City, which was seven or eight miles north of the cottage, up to the Siletz River. To cross the river it would be necessary to detour up to Highway 101, go over the bridge and down to the beach again on the other side. This would add another two or three miles so they stopped at the mouth of the river. A light purple mist hung in the December air. The sun shone mildly through, warming up the sand. It was such a warm December that they could walk without jackets. Ruby let the mild ocean breeze blow onto her shirt and face, her long hair flying freely. It was so pleasant to walk. She had the sense she could keep walking forever and never tire of it. In their dreamy conversation they invented for themselves a walking holiday, from one end of Oregon to the other, down the sands along the water all the way to California. They planned where to stop, which motels to stay in, where to rest on the way.

Jeanette brought a new bottle of Cabernet Sauvignon and then the dinners. Some kind of marinated chicken appeared in front of Ruby, a shellfull of seafood bits in white sauce before Ascott, and stuffed veal went down on Trinidad's side of the table. It was a full night at *Chez Jeanette*. All the tables were occupied by holiday-goers down at the beach for an unusual Christmas. Ruby guessed none of the guests were locals. The locals were so poor, they would never be able to afford these hundred dollar dinners. They discussed reasons for the poverty in the area as they nibbled at the food. Ascott claimed fishing, the main industry here, was not lucrative to begin with and fishing stocks were on the decline as well. The other main industry was lumber, and competition with the Canadians left local lumber companies without business. As they talked, Ruby noticed how dim and yellow the light in the restaurant was. The huge fireplace, opposite from their table, crackled with immense burning logs that a young man with a hooked nose kept putting in. She sat next to the window and suddenly Felix the cat was standing on the flower box, packed full of bright red geraniums, looking intently through the glass at her piece of chicken.

It was their last evening on the coast. She looked at her mother across from her declaring something to Ascott she wasn't listening to, her cheeks a little red from the wine. And her brother, nodding in affectionate affirmation, adding little comments. No matter how much he drank, Ruby had never in her life seen him *drunk*. Not even a slight bit inebriated. Would she have had such a nice evening if she had stayed home? Could she have been so *wrong* to have wanted to refuse to come? The image of the doorknob kept popping up in her mind: the object of our energies, says Robert Bly, is to get the doorknob from the *outside* of the door, where other people have access to it and you don't, to the *inside* of the door, where only you can open and close accessibility to your life. That was fine as far as it went. *But how can you be sure you always know when to open the door and when to close it?* The problem is not so simple. It is one thing to take control of your life, another to make decisions. It is possible to be *pleasantly surprised*. It is possible to make mistakes.

After dinner they walked back to the cottage, a mile away. It was a beautiful night. Stars stood bright and clear in the pitch-black heaven and the rumbling of the ocean could be heard in the distance. Ascott and Ruby decided to take a look at the ocean and went on down the path that took them towards the beach. A weather-worn iron staircase hung on the cliff and they looked for it in the darkness. No light shone anywhere and they were forced to use their night sight and the moon. When they found the stairs they groped for the hand-rail. It would be so easy to fall and break one's neck on these stairs. But they managed to get down onto the sand and thread their way through barnacle-covered rocks to the wet sand where ocean ripples flooded over at irregular intervals.

They stood still and watched the immense ocean in the night. The rumbling, thundering noise carried twice as heavily at night. Against the backdrop of the black horizon, white mountains of foam that consti-tuted huge waves appeared and stampeded towards them with the force of a thousand steam engines. In the distance a little light could be seen alone out on the sea. "A fishing boat," Ascott pointed out. Far towards the south another light showed a lighthouse. That boat was so alone in such a huge space. Nothing but water — absolutely black, tar-like water — everywhere around them. Ruby was surprised by the immensity of everything. At night the ocean was not beautiful. It was onerous. Almost frightening. She thought of the times she had sailed as a child: when the ship undulated on the black water, as black as oil, and the engine hummed everywhere, in the walls, under the bunk, behind the sink in the cabin. Only that engine kept them out of the enveloping grasp of the ocean itself. She was over-awed and in a way she had not yet figured out, the fear the ocean at night inspired in her was the source of her security. The warm ocean that was like a mother's embrace.

For the first time since arriving, Ruby had a sense of her father's presence as she and Ascott stood silently on the sand facing the sea. She had not allowed herself to think of him. But here, in front of the water, it was all right. Her father's spirit was somehow there: not in an intimate way. He seemed far away and completely helpless, but not in pain and not in sorrow. He was watching them from an immense distance through which nothing living could transpire. It was not a sense of God or eternity or any of the notions she had been taught. But an intimation of *nature*. A sensation that *everything that happens is natural*. There was nothing here that was not part of nature. And in a way, no matter what decisions she made in life, it would all come to the same end.

They turned back when they were starting to feel the night cold creep under their skin. Finding their way to the iron stairs, they crawled up off the sand and walked back to the cottage where Trinidad was keeping a fire going in the cone fireplace she had purchased from Gleneden Brick Works down the road. "How was it?" Trinidad called out as soon as they entered. "Fine down there," Ascott answered hanging up his jacket. Ruby took off her sandy and wet shoes and put them on the electric radiator. She hung her sweater up on a hook in the kitchen. When she came back to the living room she sat down beside Trinidad in front of the fire to warm up. "How was the beach?" her mother asked affectionately. Ruby looked at her dark skin glowing in the flames. "It was nice," she answered. "Really, quite nice."

Acknowledgements

The author wishes to thank the University of Alberta for the opportunity to put this book together as Writer-in-Residence, 1989-90.

"The Guest House" first appeared in *Canadian Fiction Magazine*. 1990.

"Water" first appeared in *The Massachusetts Review*. Spring, 1990.

"The Empty Schoolroom" first appeared in *Canadian Forum*. October, 1990.

"Sorrow Cow" first appeared in *North Dakota Quarterly*. 1992.

"Mass and a Dance" first appeared in Begamudre, Ven & J. Krause, Ed. *Out of Place*. Regina, SK: Coteau Books, 1991, and was a finalist in the CBC Literary Competitions for Fiction for 1989.

"Insomnia" first appeared in an earlier version in Gunnars, K., Ed. *Unexpected Fictions: New Icelandic Canadian Writing*. Winnipeg, MB: Turnstone Press, 1989.

"The Song of the Reindeer" first appeared in an earlier version in Magnússon, S.A., Ed. *Icelandic Writing Today*. Reykjavik, Iceland. 1982.